"You're risking your life because of me. I have to be able to do the same for you."

"That's the last thing I want—"

"Too bad, because that's the way it is," Maggie said and stepped to him, standing on tiptoes. Her lips brushed across his cheek like a sweet whisper, sending sparks shooting along his nerve endings.

He flinched and stepped back.

"Sorry," she said, looking both surprised and confused.

"You shocked me, that's all. Static electricity, you know." He could see the lie reflected in her gaze.

No woman had ever affected Jesse like this. He told himself it was because he couldn't have her. Might never be able to have her. But he knew it was a hell of a lot more than that or his heart wouldn't ache the way it did at the thought.

Dear Harlequin Intrigue Reader,

As you make travel plans for the summer, don't forget to pack along this month's exciting new Harlequin Intrigue books!

The notion of being able to rewrite history has always been fascinating, so be sure to check out *Secret Passage* by Amanda Stevens. In this wildly innovative third installment in QUANTUM MEN, supersoldier Zac Riley must complete a vital mission, but his long-lost love is on a crucial mission of her own! Opposites combust in *Wanted Woman* by B.J. Daniels, which pits a beautiful daredevil on the run against a fiercely protective deputy sheriff—the next book in CASCADES CONCEALED.

Julie Miller revisits THE TAYLOR CLAN when one of Kansas City's finest infiltrates a crime boss's compound and finds himself under the dangerous spell of an aristocratic beauty. Will he be the *Last Man Standing?* And in *Legally Binding* by Ann Voss Peterson—the second sizzling story in our female-driven in-line continuity SHOTGUN SALLYS—a reformed bad boy rancher needs the help of the best female legal eagle in Texas to clear him of murder!

Who can resist those COWBOY COPS? In our latest offering in our Western-themed promotion, Adrianne Lee tantalizes with *Denim Detective*. This gripping family-in-jeopardy tale has a small-town sheriff riding to the rescue, but he's about to learn one doozy of a secret.... And finally this month you are cordially invited to partake in *Her Royal Bodyguard* by Joyce Sullivan, an enchanting mystery about a commoner who discovers she's a betrothed princess and teams up with an enigmatic bodyguard who vows to protect her from evildoers.

Enjoy our fabulous lineup this month!

Sincerely,

Denise O'Sullivan
Senior Editor, Harlequin Intrigue

WANTED WOMAN

B.J. DANIELS

TORONTO • NEW YORK • LONDON
AMSTERDAM • PARIS • SYDNEY • HAMBURG
STOCKHOLM • ATHENS • TOKYO • MILAN • MADRID
PRAGUE • WARSAW • BUDAPEST • AUCKLAND

ISBN 0-373-22778-7

WANTED WOMAN

This edition published by arrangement with Harlequin Books S.A.

www.eHarlequin.com

Printed in U.S.A.

ABOUT THE AUTHOR

A former award-winning journalist, B.J. Daniels had thirty-six short stories published before her first romantic suspense, *Odd Man Out*, came out in 1995. Her book *Premeditated Marriage* won the *Romantic Times* Best Intrigue award for 2002 and she received a Career Achievement Award for Romantic Suspense. B.J. lives in Montana with her husband, Parker, three springer spaniels, Zoey, Scout and Spot, and a temperamental tomcat named Jeff. She is a member of Kiss of Death, the Bozeman Writers' Group and Romance Writers of America. When she isn't writing, she snowboards in the winters and camps, water-skis and plays tennis in the summers. All year she plays her favorite sport, tennis. To contact her, write P.O. Box 183, Bozeman, MT 59771 or look for her online at www.bjdaniels.com.

Books by B.J. Daniels

HARLEQUIN INTRIGUE

312—ODD MAN OUT
353—OUTLAWED!
417—HOTSHOT P.I.
446—UNDERCOVER CHRISTMAS
493—A FATHER FOR HER BABY
533—STOLEN MOMENTS
555—LOVE AT FIRST SIGHT
566—INTIMATE SECRETS
585—THE AGENT'S SECRET CHILD
604—MYSTERY BRIDE
617—SECRET BODYGUARD
643—A WOMAN WITH A MYSTERY
654—HOWLING IN THE DARKNESS
687—PREMEDITATED MARRIAGE
716—THE MASKED MAN
744—MOUNTAIN SHERIFF*
761—DAY OF RECKONING*
778—WANTED WOMAN*

*Cascades Concealed

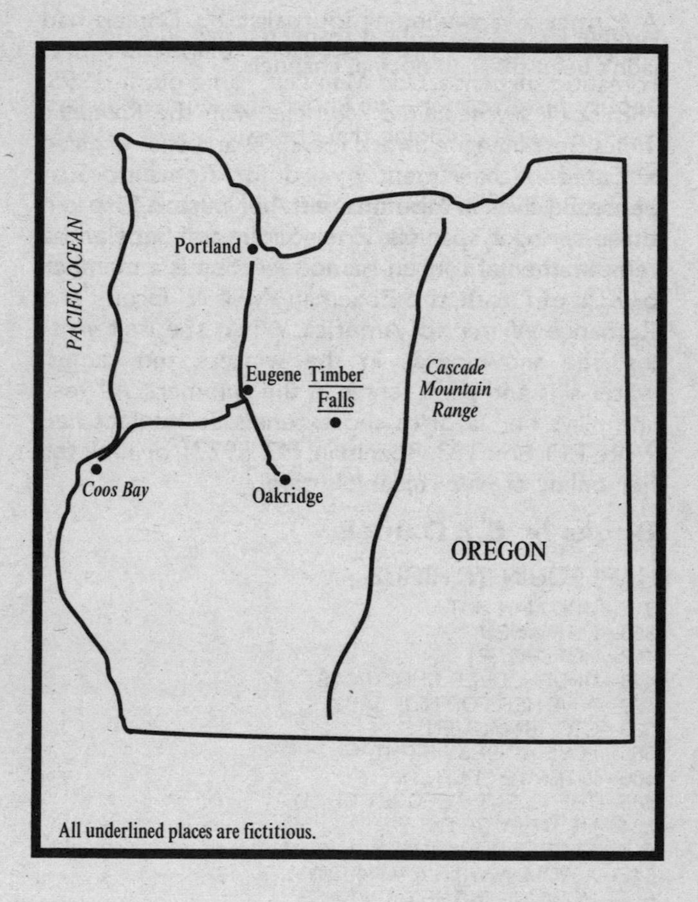
PACIFIC OCEAN
Portland
Eugene
Timber Falls
Cascade Mountain Range
Coos Bay
Oakridge
OREGON
All underlined places are fictitious.

CAST OF CHARACTERS

Maggie Randolph—She'd suspected her adoption hadn't been through normal channels.

Deputy Jesse Tanner—He knows the moment he lays eyes on Maggie Randolph that she is in trouble—and so is he.

Detective Rupert Blackmore—All he wants is to retire, buy an RV and spend winters in Arizona playing shuffleboard. But first he has to tie up a few loose ends.

Norman Drake—The legal assistant gets caught napping on the job—and witnesses a murder.

Clark Iverson—The lawyer wants to make things right, and it costs him his life.

Wade and Daisy Dennison—Both lied about the night their daughter Angela was kidnapped twenty-seven years ago.

Mitch Tanner—The Timber Falls sheriff is recuperating from two gunshot wounds so his older brother Jesse is in charge.

Charity Jenkins—Her snooping could get her killed.

Lydia Abernathy—The antique-shop owner says the new man in town has been casing her joint. Or does she have ulterior motives for putting Charity on the story?

Angus Smythe—The Englishman has been taking care of Lydia for years—ever since the car accident that left her in a wheelchair. But is his interest romantic or financial?

Jerome Bruno Lovelace—The small-time crook is romancing the owner of Betty's Café.

Ruth Anne Tanner—She left her two sons and husband years ago and didn't look back.

This book is gratefully dedicated to
the Bozeman Writers' Group for all their wonderful
support and encouragement. Thank you, Randle, Wenda,
Kitty, Bob, LuAnn and Mark. You're the best!

Chapter One

Puget Sound, Seattle

The smell of fish and sea rolled up off the dark water on the late-night air. Restless waves from the earlier storm crashed into pilings under the pier and in the distance a horn groaned through the thick fog.

Maggie shut off the motorcycle and coasted through the shadows and damp fog. She couldn't see a thing But she figured that was good since he wouldn't be able to see her. Nor hear her coming.

She'd dressed in her black leathers and boots. Even the bulging bike saddlebag was black as the night. She told herself she was being paranoid as she hid the bike and walked several blocks through the dark old warehouses and fish plants before she started down the long pier.

He would be waiting for her somewhere on the pier. With the dense fog and the crashing surf, she wouldn't know where until she was practically on top of him. She assured herself that she had taken every precaution—short of bringing a weapon.

But she was no fool. He had the advantage. He'd picked the meeting place. He was expecting her. And because of the fog, she wouldn't know what was waiting for her at the end of the deserted pier until she reached it.

Fortunately, she was a woman used to taking chances. Except tonight, the stakes were higher than they'd ever been.

The sound of the sea breaking against the pilings grew louder and louder, the wet fog thicker and blinding white. She knew she had to be nearing the end of the pier.

And suddenly Norman Drake materialized out of the fog.

He looked like hell. Like a man who'd been on the run from the police for three days. He looked scared and dangerous—right down to the gun he had clutched in his right hand.

He waved it at her, his pale blue eyes wide with alarm. And she wondered where he'd gotten the gun and if he knew how to use it. He was young and smart and completely out of his league—a tall, thin, bookworm turned law student turned law assistant. She could smell the nervous sweat coming off him, the fear.

"You alone?" he whispered hoarsely.

She nodded.

"You sure you weren't followed?"

"Positive."

He exhaled loudly and wiped his free hand over his mouth. "You bring the money?"

She nodded. The ten thousand dollars he'd demanded weighted down the saddlebag. She reached in slowly and held up one bundle. Unmarked, all old, small denomination bills, dozens of bundles making the bag bulge.

It took him a minute to lower the weapon. His hands shook as he shoved it into the front waistband of his wrinkled, soiled slacks. Not a good idea under any circumstances. As nervous as he was, he'd shoot his nuts off.

"I didn't know who else to call but you," he said, his gaze jumping back and forth between her and the fogged-in pier behind her. "They killed Iverson and they'll kill me, too, if I don't get out of town."

Clark Iverson, her father's long-time attorney, had been murdered three days ago. The police had determined that his temporary student legal assistant was in the building at the time. There was no sign of forced entry. No sign of a struggle. Visitors had to be buzzed in. That's why the cops were actively looking for Norman.

"You told me on the phone you had important information for me about my father's plane crash," she said, keeping her hand clamped on the saddlebag, keeping her tone neutral.

He nodded, a jittery nod that set her teeth on edge. "It wasn't an accident. The same person who murdered Iverson killed your father."

She felt shock ricochet through her. Then disbelief. "It was determined an accident. Pilot failure."

Norman shook his head. "A week before the crash, your father came into the office. He seemed upset.

Later, after he left, I overheard Iverson on the phone telling someone he couldn't talk your dad out of it."

"That's not enough evidence—"

"I was there three nights ago, I heard them talking about the plane crash. Iverson had figured out that the plane had gone down to keep your father from talking. He threatened to go to the Feds. I heard them kill him—" Emotion choked off the last of his words.

"You actually heard someone admit to murdering my father?"

He nodded, his Adam's apple going up and down, up and down. She watched him, shock and pain and anger mixing with the grief of the past two months since the single passenger plane had gone down on a routine business flight. She fought to keep her voice calm. "You said *they?*"

He seemed surprised by the question. "Did I? I only heard one man talk but—" He frowned and looked away. "I remember thinking I heard two people coming down the hall after the elevator opened." He was lying and doing a poor job of it. Why lie about how many killers there were? "You believe me, don't you?"

She didn't know what to believe now. But her father had liked Norman, thought he was going to make a good lawyer someday. Good lawyer, an oxymoron if there ever was one, her father would have joked. "Norman, how did they get in? The building was locked, right?"

He nodded, looking confused. "I guess Iverson buzzed them up. All I know is that I heard the elevator and—" He looked behind her again as if he'd heard something. "I somehow knew not to let them know I was there."

A foghorn let out a mournful moan from out beyond the city.

"You're telling me Clark didn't *know* you were still in the office?"

Norman fidgeted. "I'd fallen asleep in the library doing some research for him. The door to his office was closed. Earlier, he'd told me to leave, to do the rest in the morning. I guess he thought I'd left by the door to the hallway. The elevator woke me, then I heard voices arguing."

Just seconds before he'd said he'd heard two sets of footsteps coming down the hall after the elevator opened. No wonder Norman hadn't gone to the police. His story had so many holes it wouldn't even make good Swiss cheese.

"You heard them arguing?" she asked.

He nodded. "Then I heard this like...grunt and glass breaking—" He closed his eyes as if imagining Clark Iverson's body, the lamp he'd grabbed as he went down shattered on the floor next to him, his eyes open staring blindly upward, a knife sticking out of his chest at heart level, just as he'd looked when his secretary and Maggie had found him the next morning. Just as he must have looked when Norman saw him.

"You didn't see the killer."

"No, I told you, I just ran."

"Why didn't you call the police?" It was the same question the cops wanted to ask him.

Norman closed his eyes tightly as if in pain. "After they killed him, they rummaged around in his desk drawers, in his file cabinets. I could hear them. I was afraid that at any minute they'd come into the library and find me.'' Another look away, another lie. ''I just ran. I took the stairs, let myself out the back way and I've been running ever since. If they find me, they'll kill me.''

''Did you recognize the one voice you heard?''

He shook his head.

''But you heard what were they arguing about.''

''Iverson said the secret wasn't worth killing people over.''

''What secret?''

Norman squirmed, his gaze flicking past her. ''An illegal adoption.''

She felt a chill come off the ocean as if she already knew what his next words would be.

''You were the baby,'' Norman said, the words tumbling over themselves in their struggle to get out. ''Iverson wanted to tell you the truth. That's why they killed him. He said your father had found out and was going to tell you.''

''Found out what?'' So her parents hadn't gone through the proper channels. So what? ''I'm twenty-seven years old. Why would anyone kill over my adoption no matter how it went down?''

''It was the way you were...acquired,'' Norman said. ''Your father had found out that you were kidnapped.''

Kidnapped? She'd always known she was adopted and that was the reason she looked nothing like her parents. Nor was anything like them.

Mildred and Paul Randolph had always seemed a

little surprised by their only child, a little leery. Maggie had come into their life after they'd tried numerous adoption agencies, they'd told her. She'd been a miracle, they'd said. A gift from God.

Maybe not quite.

Although well-off financially, her parents weren't the ideal adoptive candidates. Her mother had been confined to a wheelchair since childhood polio and her father was considered too old. He'd been fifty when Maggie had come along. But, according to both Mildred and Paul, they'd finally found an agency that understood how desperately they wanted a child and had given Maggie to them to love.

No child could have asked for more loving parents. But they'd been horribly overprotective, so afraid something would happen to her, that Maggie had become fearless in self-defense. By the age of twenty-seven, she'd tried everything from skydiving and bungie jumping to motorcross, heli-skiing and speedboat racing.

Her parents had been terrified. Now she realized they'd been afraid long before their only child had become a thrill-seeker. Now she knew why she'd seen fear in her father's eyes all of her life. He'd been waiting all these years for the other shoe to drop.

It had finally dropped. He'd found out she was kidnapped and couldn't live with the knowledge.

She heard a board creak behind her, heavy with a tentative step. ''Norman, you have to tell the police what you told me. They'll protect you.''

''Are you *nuts?* You can't trust anyone. These people have already killed twice to keep their secret. Who knows how influential they are or what connections they might have.''

He'd seen the killer and knew something he wasn't telling her. That's why he was so afraid. Well, maybe the cops could get the truth out of him. ''Norman, I called the detective on the case after I talked to you. Detective Blackmore.''

''What?'' He looked around wildly. ''Don't you realize what you've done?'' He grabbed for the saddlebag. ''Give me the money. I have to get out of here. Quick. He'll kill us both if—'' Norman broke off, his gaze riveted on something just over her left shoulder, eyes widening in horror.

She heard the soft pop, didn't recognize the sound until she saw blood bloom across the shoulder of Norman's jacket. The second shot—right on the heels of the first—caught him in the chest, dead-on.

His grip on the saddlebag pulled her down with him as he fell to the weathered boards, dropping her to her knees beside him.

''Oh, Norman. Oh, God.'' Her mind reeled. The police wouldn't have shot him. Not without a warning first. But who else had known about their meeting?

The third shot sent a shaft of pain tearing through her left arm as she tried to free herself of the saddlebag strap and Norman's death grip.

''Timber Falls,'' he whispered, blood running from the corner of his mouth as his fingers released the bag of money and her. ''That's where they got you.'' Adding on his last breath, ''Run.''

But there was no place to run. She was trapped. Behind her, she heard the groan of a board, caught the scent of the killer on the breeze, a nauseating mix of perspiration, cheap cologne and stale cigar smoke.

She had only one choice. She fell over Norman, rolling him with her, using his body as a shield as a fourth shot thudded into his dead body.

As she fell, she looked up, saw the man with the gun come out of the fog. Shock paralyzed her as her eyes met his and she realized she knew him.

She let out a cry as he raised the gun and pulled the trigger. Two more shots thudded into Norman's riddled body as she rolled off the end of the pier taking Norman and the saddlebag with her, dropping for what seemed an eternity before plunging into the cold, dark roiling water below.

Chapter Two

Outside Timber Falls, Oregon

Jesse Tanner had been restless for days. He stood on his deck, looking down the steep timbered mountain into the darkness, wishing for sleep. It had been raining earlier. Wisps of clouds scooted by on a light breeze.

He sniffed the cedar-scented air as if he could smell trouble, sense danger, find something to explain the restlessness that haunted his nights and gave him no peace.

But whatever was bothering him it remained as illusive as slumber.

A sound drew him from his thoughts. A recognizable throaty rumble. He looked toward the break in the trees below him on the steep mountain to the strip of pavement that was only visible in daylight. Or for those few moments when headlights could be seen at night on the isolated stretch of highway below him.

The single light came out of the trees headed in the

direction of Timber Falls. A biker, moving fast, the throb of the big cycle echoing up to him.

Jesse watched the motorcycle glide like warm butter over the wet, dark pavement and wished that he was on it, headed wherever, destination unknown.

But that was the old Jesse Tanner. This Jesse was through wandering. Through with the open road. This Jesse had settled down.

Not that he still couldn't envy the biker below him on the highway. Or remember that heady feeling of speed and darkness and freedom. There was nothing like it late at night when he had the road to himself. Just an endless ribbon of black pavement stretched in front of him and infinite possibilities just over the next rise.

He started to turn away but a set of headlights flickered in the trees as a car came roaring out of a side road across the highway below him. He watched, frozen in horror as the car tore out of Maple Creek Road and onto to the highway—directly into the path of the motorcycle.

He caught a flash of bright red in the headlamp of the bike and saw the car, a convertible, the top down and the dark hair of the woman behind the wheel blowing back in that instant before the bike collided with the side of the car, clipping it. The bike and rider went down.

Jesse gripped the railing as the bike slid on its side down the pavement, sparks flying as the car sped away into the darkness and trees, headed toward Timber Falls, five miles away.

He was already running for his old pickup he kept

for getting firewood. Other than that, all he had was his Harley. Taking off down his jeep trail of a road in the truck, he dropped down the face of the mountain, fearing what he'd find when he reached the pavement.

At the highway, he turned north. It was darker down here with the forest towering on each side of the two-lane. In the slit of sky overhead, clouds scudded past, giving only brief glimpses of stars and a silver sliver of moon.

He hadn't gone far when he spotted the fallen bike in his headlights. It lay on its side in the ditch, the single headlamp casting a stationary beam of gold across the wet highway. Where was the biker?

Driving slowly up the road, he scanned the path with his headlights looking for the downed rider, bracing himself for what he'd find.

A dozen yards back up the highway from the bike, something gleamed in his headlights. The shiny top of a bike helmet. The biker lay on his side at the edge of the road, unmoving.

Jesse swore and stopped, turning on his emergency flashers to block any traffic that might come along. He didn't expect any given the time of the night—or the season. Early spring—the rainy season in this part of the country. People with any sense stayed clear of the Pacific side of the Cascades where, at this time of year, two hundred inches of rain fell pretty much steadily for seven months. The ones who lived here just tried not to go crazy during the rainy season. Some didn't succeed.

Following the beams of his headlights, he jumped out of the pickup and ran across the wet pavement toward the biker, unconsciously calculating the odds that the guy was still alive, already debating whether to get him into the back of the truck and run him to the hospital or not move him and go for help.

As he neared, he heard a soft moan and saw movement as the biker came around. Jesse figured he was witnessing a miracle given how fast the motorcycle had been traveling.

"Take it easy," he said as the figure in all black leathers coughed as if gasping for breath and tried to sit up. The biker was small, slim and a damned lucky dude.

As Jesse knelt down beside him in the glow of the pickup's headlights, he saw with shock that he'd been wrong and let out an oath as a hand with recently manicured nails pulled off the helmet. A full head of long dark curly hair tumbled out and a distinctly female voice said, "I'm okay."

"Holy..." he said rocking back on his heels. This was one damned lucky...*chick.*

She had her head down as if a little groggy.

He watched her test each leg, then each arm. "Are you sure you're not hurt?" He couldn't believe everything was working right. "Nothing's broken?"

She shook her head, still bent over as if trying to catch her breath.

He waited, amazed as he took in the leather-clad body. Amazed by the bod and the bike. She was wheeling a forty-thousand-dollar ride that most men couldn't handle. A hell of a bike for a girl. It was too heavy for anyone but an expert rider. No wonder she'd been able to dump the bike and not get hurt.

She tried to get up again.

''Give it another minute. No hurry,'' he said, looking from her, back up the highway to her bike. This gal had nine lives, a whole lot of luck and she knew how to ride that fancy bike. He wasn't sure what impressed him more.

''I'm all right.'' Her voice surprised him. It was all female, cultured and educated-sounding and in stark contrast to her getup and her chosen mode of transportation.

But the real shocker was when she lifted her head, flipping back her hair, and he saw her face.

All the air went out of him as if she'd sucker punched him. ''Sweet Mother—'' he muttered, rearing back again. She was breathtaking. Her skin was the color of warm honey sprinkled with cinnamon and sugar freckles across high cheekbones. And her eyes... They were wide and the color of cedar, warm and rich. She was exquisite. A natural beauty.

And there was something almost familiar about her...

She tried to get to her feet, bringing him out of his dumbfounded inertia.

''Here, let me help you,'' he said and reached under her armpits to lift her to her feet. She was amazingly light and small next to him.

She accepted his help with grace and gratitude even though it was clear she liked doing things for herself.

She took a step. ''Ouch,'' she said under her breath and swayed a little on her feet.

''What is it?''

''My left ankle. It's just sprained.''

Maybe. Maybe not. "I'll take you to the hospital emergency room to see a doctor."

She shook her head. "Just get me to my bike."

"It's not rideable." He'd seen enough twisted metal on it even in passing to know that. "I'll load it into my pickup. There's not a bike shop for a hundred miles but I've worked on a few of my own. I might be able to fix it."

She looked up at him then as if seeing him for the first time. Her eyes narrowed as she took in the boots, jeans, bike rally T-shirt and his long dark ponytail. Her gaze settled on the single gold ring in his earlobe. "You live around here?"

"Right up that mountain," he said, pointing to the light he'd left on. It glowed faintly high up the mountainside.

She studied it. Then him.

It was three in the morning but he had to ask. "Is anyone expecting you up the road, anyone who'll be worried about you? Because I don't have a phone yet."

She didn't seem to hear him. "You have ice for my ankle at your place?"

He nodded.

"Good. That's all I need."

"I have a clean bed you're welcome to for what's left of the night," he offered.

She flashed him an in-your-dreams look.

He smiled and shook his head. "All I'm offering is a bed. Maybe something to eat or drink. Some ice. Nothing more."

She cocked her head at him, looking more curious

than anything else. He wondered what she saw. Whatever it was, he must have looked harmless enough before she started to limp toward her bike. "I need my saddlebag."

"I'll get it," he said catching up to her and offering a hand. "No reason to walk on that ankle any more than you have to." She quirked an eyebrow at him but said nothing as she slipped one arm around his shoulder and let him take her weight as she hobbled to the pickup.

As he opened the passenger-side door and slid her into his old truck, he felt way too damned chivalrous. Also a little embarrassed by his old truck.

She glanced around the cab, then settled back into the seat and closed her eyes. He slammed the door and went to load her bike.

He'd only seen a couple of these bikes. Too expensive for most riders. It definitely made him wonder about the woman in his pickup. The bike didn't look like it was hurt bad. He figured he should be able to fix it. He liked the idea of working on it. The bike intrigued him almost as much as the woman who'd been riding it.

He rolled the bike up the plank he kept in the back of his pickup, retrieved her saddlebag and, slamming the tailgate, went around to climb into the cab of the truck beside her. He set the heavy, bulging saddlebag on the seat beside them.

She cracked an eyelid to see that the bag was there, then closed her eyes again.

"The name's Jesse. Jesse Tanner."

She didn't move, didn't open her eyes. "Maggie," she said but offered no more.

He started the engine, shifted into first gear and headed back up the mountain to his new place. The road was steep and rough, but he liked being a little inaccessible. He saw her grimace a couple of times as he took the bumps, but she didn't open her eyes until he parked in front of the cabin.

She looked up at the structure on the hillside, only the living-room light glowing in the darkness.

"This is where you live?" she said and, opening her door, got out, slipping the saddlebag over her shoulder protectively.

Something in her tone made him wonder if she meant the cabin or the isolated location. The only visitors he'd had so far were his younger brother, Mitch, and his dad. He figured if he wanted to be social, he knew the way to town and it was only five miles. Not nearly far enough some days.

He looked at the cabin, trying to see it through her eyes. It was tall and narrow, a crude place, built of logs and recycled cedar but he was proud of it since he'd designed and built it over the winter with the help of his dad and brother. It had gone up fast.

Three stories, the first the living room and kitchen, the second a bedroom and bath with a screened in deck where he planned to sleep come summer, the third his studio, a floor flanked with windows, the view incredible.

Unfortunately, it was pretty much a shell. He hadn't furnished the inside yet. Hadn't had time. So all he had was the minimal furniture he'd picked up.

Lately, he'd been busy getting some paintings ready for an exhibit in June, his first, and— He started to tell her all of that, but stopped himself. It wasn't like she would be here more than a few hours and then she'd be gone. She didn't want his life history, he could see that from her expression.

He'd been there himself. No roots. No desire to grow any. Especially no desire to be weighed down even with someone's life story.

She was standing beside the pickup staring up at his cabin as he climbed out of the truck.

"It's still under construction," he said irritated with himself for wanting her to like it. But hell, she *was* the first woman he'd had up here since it was built.

"It's perfect," she said. "Neoclassical, right?"

He smiled, surprised at her knowledge of architecture. But then again, she was riding a forty-thousand-dollar bike and had another couple grand in leather on her back, spoke like she'd been to finishing school and carried herself as if she knew her way around the streets. All of that came from either education, money or experience. In her case, he wondered if it wasn't all three.

She caught him admiring the way her leathers fit her.

"Let's get you inside," he said quickly. "You hungry?"

She shook her head and grabbed the railing, limping up the steps to the first floor, making it clear she didn't need his help.

"You sure you don't want to see a doctor? I could run you into town—"

"No." Her tone didn't leave any doubt.

"Okay." He'd had to try.

They'd reached the front door. She seemed surprised it wasn't locked. "I haven't much to steal and most thieves are too lazy to make the trek up here." He swung the door open and she stepped inside, her gaze going at once to his paintings he'd done of his years in Mexico.

He had a half dozen leaning against the bare living-room wall waiting to go to the framer for the exhibit. She limped over to them, staring at one and then another.

"How about coffee?" he offered, uncomfortable with the way she continued to study his work as if she were seeing something in the paintings he didn't want exposed.

He couldn't decide if she liked them or not. He wasn't about to ask. He had a feeling she might tell him.

While she'd been studying the paintings he'd been studying her. As she shrugged out of her jacket, he saw that she wore a short-sleeved white T-shirt that molded her breasts and the muscles of her back. She was in good shape and her body was just as exquisite as he'd thought it would be beneath the leather.

But what stole his attention was the hole he'd seen in the jacket just below her left shoulder—and the corresponding fresh wound on her left biceps. He'd seen enough gunshot wounds in his day to recognize one even without the telltale hole in the leather jacket.

The bullet had grazed her flesh and would leave a scar. It wasn't her first scar though. There was another one on her right forearm, an older one that had required stitches.

Who the hell was this woman and what was it about her?

"These are all yours," she said, studying the paintings again. It was a statement of fact as if there was no doubt in her mind that he'd painted them.

"I have tea if you don't like coffee."

"Do you have anything stronger?" she asked without turning around.

He lifted a brow behind her back and went to the cupboard. "I have some whiskey." He turned to find her glancing around the cabin. Her gaze had settled on an old rocker he'd picked up at a flea market in Portland.

"That chair is pretty comfortable if you'd like to sit down," he said, as he watched her run her fingers over the oak arm of the antique rocker.

She looked at him as she turned and lowered herself into the rocker, obviously trying hard not to let him see that her ankle was hurting her if not the rest of her body. Maybe nothing was broken but she'd been beat up. Wait until tomorrow. She was going to be hurtin' for certain.

He handed her half a glass of whiskey. He poured himself a tall glass of lemonade. The whiskey had been a housewarming gift from a well-meaning friend in town. He'd given up alcohol when he'd decided it was time to settle down. He'd seen what alcohol had done for his old man and he'd never *needed* the stuff, especially now that he was painting again.

He watched Maggie over the rim of his glass as he

took a drink. He'd made the lemonade from real lemons. It wasn't half-bad. Could use a little more sugar though.

She sniffed the whiskey, then drained the glass and grimaced, nose wrinkling, as if she'd just downed paint thinner. Then she pushed herself to her feet, limped over to him and handed him the glass. "Thank you."

"Feeling better?" he asked, worried about her and not just because of her bike wreck.

"Fine."

He nodded, doubting it. He wanted to ask her how she'd gotten the bullet wound, what she'd been doing on the highway below his place at three in the morning, where she was headed and what kind of trouble she was in. But he knew better. He'd been there and he wasn't that far from that life that he didn't know how she would react to even well-meaning questions.

"I promised you icc," he said and finished his lemonade, then put their glasses in the sink and filled a plastic bag with ice cubes for her ankle. "And a place to lie down while I take a look at your bike." He met her gaze. She still wasn't sure about him.

He realized just how badly he wanted her to trust him as he gazed into those brown eyes. Like her face, there was something startlingly familiar about them.

She took the bag of ice cubes and he led her up the stairs, stopping at his bedroom door.

"You can have this room. The sheets are clean." He hadn't slept on them since he'd changed them.

"No, that one's yours," she said and turned toward the open doorway to the screened-in deck. There was an old futon out there and a pine dresser he planned to refinish when he had time. "I'll sleep in here."

He started to argue, but without turning on the light, she took the bag of ice and limped over to the screened windows, her back to him as she looked out into the darkness beyond.

Fetching a towel from the bathroom, he returned to find her still standing at the window. She didn't turn when he put the towel on the futon, just said, "Thank you."

"*De nada.*" He was struck with the thought that if he had been able to sleep he would never have seen her accident, would never have met her. For some reason that seemed important as if cosmically it had all been planned. He was starting to think like his future sister-in-law Charity and her crazy aunt Florie, the self-proclaimed psychic.

He really needed to get some decent sleep, he concluded wryly, if he was going to start thinking crap like that. "There are sheets and blankets in the dresser and more towels in the bathroom." He would have gladly made a bed for her but he knew instinctively that she needed to be alone.

"About my bike—"

"I think I can fix it," he said. "Otherwise, I can give you and the bike a lift into Eugene."

She turned then to frown at him. "You'd do that?"

He nodded. "I used to travel a lot on my bike and people helped me. Payback. I need the karma." He smiled.

Her expression softened with her smile. She really was exquisite. For some reason, he thought of Desiree

Dennison, the woman he'd seen driving the red sports car that had hit Maggie. "I can also take you in to see the sheriff in the morning. I know him pretty well."

"Why would I want to see him?" she asked, frowning and looking leery again.

"You'll want to press charges against the driver of the car that hit you."

She said nothing, but he saw the answer in her eyes. No chance in hell was she sticking around to press charges against anyone.

"Just give a holler if you need anything," he said.

Her gaze softened again and for an instant he thought he glimpsed vulnerability. The instant passed. "Thank you again for everything."

My pleasure. He left the bathroom door open and a light on so she could find it if she needed it, then went downstairs, smiling as he recalled the face she'd made after chugging the whiskey. Who the hell was she? Ruefully, he realized the chances were good that he would never know.

MAGGIE HURT ALL OVER. She put the ice down on the futon and limped closer to the screened window. The night air was damp and cool, but not cold.

She stared out, still shaken by what had happened on the dock, what she'd learned, what she'd witnessed. She'd gotten Norman killed because she'd called Detective Rupert Blackmore.

Below, a door opened and closed. She watched Jesse Tanner cross the mountainside to a garage, open the door and turn on the light. An older classic Harley was parked inside, the garage neat and clean.

She watched from the darkness as he went to the truck, dropped the tailgate, pulled out the plank, then climbed up and carefully rolled her bike down and over to the garage.

For a long moment he stood back as if admiring the cycle, then slowly he approached it. She caught her breath as he ran his big hands over it, gentle hands, caressing the bike the way a man caressed a woman he cherished.

She moved away from the window, letting the night air slow her throbbing pulse and cool the heat that burned across her bare skin. She told herself it was the effects of the whiskey not the man below her window as she tried to close her mind to the feelings he evoked in her. How could she feel desire when her life was in danger?

She'd been running on adrenalin for almost thirty-six hours now, too keyed up to sleep or eat. Her stomach growled but she knew she needed rest more than food at this point. She could hear the soft clink of tools in the garage, almost feel the warm glow of the light drifting up to her.

She took a couple of blankets from the chest of drawers. Wrapping the towel he'd left her around the bag of ice, she curled up on the futon bed, put the ice on her ankle and pulled the blankets up over her.

The bed smelled of the forest and the night and possibly the man who lived here. She breathed it in finding a strange kind of comfort in the smell of him and the sound of him below her.

She closed her eyes tighter, just planning to rest until he was through with her bike, knowing she would never be able to sleep. Not when she was this close to Timber Falls. This close to learning the truth. Just a few more miles. A few more hours.

Tonight on the highway when the car had pulled out in front of her, she'd thought at first it was Detective Rupert Blackmore trying to kill her again.

But then she'd caught a glimpse of the female driver in that instant before she'd hit the bright red sports car.

She'd seen the young woman's startled face in the bike's headlight, seen the long dark hair and wide eyes, and as Maggie had laid the bike on its side, she'd heard the car speed off into the night all the time knowing that the cop would have never left. He would have finished her off.

She'd feared that Norman's body had washed up by now. And it was only a matter of time before Blackmore realized her body wouldn't be washing up because she hadn't drowned.

How soon would he figure out where she'd gone and what she was up to and come here to stop her?

But what was it he didn't want her finding out? That she was kidnapped? Or was there something more, something he feared even worse that she would uncover?

Right now, all she knew was that people were dying because of *her*. Because her parents had wanted a baby so desperately that they'd bought one, not knowing that she'd been kidnapped from a family in Timber Falls, Oregon.

Her ankle ached. She tried not to think. Detective

Rupert Blackmore was bound to follow her to Timber Falls. Unless he was already in town waiting for her.

Sleep came like a dark black cloak that enveloped her. She didn't see the fog or Norman lying dead at her feet or the cop on the pier with the gun coming after her. And for a while, she felt safe.

Chapter Three

Maggie woke with a start, her heart pounding. Her eyes flew open but she stayed perfectly still, listening for the thing she feared most.

The creak of a floorboard nearby. The soft rustle of clothing. The sound of a furtive breath taken and held.

She heard nothing but the cry of a blue jay and the soft whisper of the breeze in the swaying dark pines beyond her bed.

She opened her eyes surprised to see that the soft pale hues of dawn had lightened the screened-in room. She'd slept. That surprised her. Obviously she'd been tired, but to sleep in a perfect stranger's house knowing there was someone out there who wanted her dead? She must have been more exhausted than she'd thought.

She listened for a moment, wondering what sound had awakened her and if it was one she needed to worry about. Silence emanated from within the house and there was no longer the soft clink of tools.

Sitting up, she retrieved the bag and towel, and swung her legs over the side of the bed. The ice she'd had on her ankle had melted. Some of the water had leaked onto the futon. The towel was soaked and cold to the touch.

She scooped up both towel and bag and pushed to her feet to test her ankle. Last night she'd been scared that her ankle was hurt badly. Anything that slowed her down would be deadly.

Her ankle was stiff and painful, but she could walk well enough. And ride. She stood on the worn wood-plank flooring and took a few tentative steps toward the screened windows. That is, she could ride if her bike was fixed.

She glanced out. The garage door was shut, the light out. The back of the pickup was empty. Her bike sat in front of the house, resting on its kickstand, her helmet sitting on top, waiting for her. He'd fixed it.

The swell of relief and gratitude that washed over her made her sway a little on her weak ankle. Tears burned her eyes. His kindness felt like too much right now. She turned toward the open doorway. She'd left her door open and so it seemed had he. As she neared the short hallway between the rooms, she could see him sleeping in his double bed, the covers thrown back, only the sheet over him.

He was curled around his pillow on his side facing her, his masculine features soft in sleep. A lock of his long straight black hair fell over one cheek, shiny and dark as a raven's wing. She caught the glint of his earring beneath the silken strands, the shadow of his strong stubbled jaw, the dark silken fringe of his eyelashes against his skin.

Even asleep the man still held her attention, still

exuded a wild sensuality, a rare sexuality. This man would be dangerous to a woman. And she didn't doubt he'd known his share. Intimately. Or that he was a good lover. She'd seen the way he'd touched her bike. She'd seen his artwork. Both had made her ache. Fear for her life hadn't stolen her most primitive desires last night. Nor this morning.

But what surprised her wasn't her attraction to the man, but that she felt safe with him. Too safe.

She moved silently down the hallway. He'd left a small light burning in the bathroom for her. That gesture even more than the others touched her deeply. She closed the door behind her and poured what water was left in the plastic bag down the drain, then hung up the towel.

She washed her face, avoiding looking at the stranger in the mirror. She'd spent too many years questioning who she was. Now she was about to find out and she didn't want to face it or what her adoptive parents might have done in their desperation for a child.

She knew money had exchanged hands. Most adoptions involved an exchange of money, although she hated to think what her parents had paid for her. What frightened her was how the purchase had been made. And why someone was now trying to kill her to keep her from finding out.

No one committed multiple murders to cover up an illegal adoption or even a kidnapping. Especially after twenty-seven years. There had to be more to it. What was someone afraid would come to light?

According to Norman, the answer was in Timber

Falls—just a few miles away now. She had raced here, running for her life, rocketing through the darkness toward the truth. But now that she was so close, she feared what she would find.

When she was younger, she'd often thought about finding her biological parents. Of course, her adoptive parents had discouraged her. Now she knew it wasn't just because they didn't want to share her.

Unfortunately, now she had no choice but to find out who she really was. And hopefully the answer would save her life. But what would her life be worth once she knew the truth?

As she turned to leave the bathroom, she froze. A sheriff deputy's uniform hung on the hook of the closed door.

THE CALL CAME before daylight. Detective Rupert Blackmore was lying on his bed, fully clothed, flat on his back, staring up at the ceiling. Certainly not asleep. He'd been waiting for the phone to ring, willing it to ring with the news he needed.

Praying for it. Although praying might not have been exactly what he'd been doing. Right now he would have sold his soul to the devil if he hadn't already traded it to Satan a long time ago.

He let the phone ring three times, then picked up the receiver. "Detective Blackmore."

"Just fished a body out of the sea near the old pier," said his subordinate, a young new detective by the name of Williams. "Six gunshot wounds. Dead before the body hit the water. Definitely a homicide."

Rupert Blackmore held his breath as he got to his feet beside the bed. "Has the body been ID-ed?"

"Affirmative. Norman Drake. Wallet was in his pocket. The guy we've been looking for in connection with the murder of his boss, attorney Clark Iverson."

As if Rupert didn't know that. He tried not to let Williams hear his disappointment that Norman's body was the only one found so far. "Close off the entire area. I want it searched thoroughly. Drake didn't act alone and now it appears there's been a falling out among murderers."

He hung up and cursed, then in a fit of rage and frustration, knocked the phone off the nightstand, sending it crashing to the floor.

He sat down on the edge of the bed and lowered his head to his hands. Her body would wash up. Then all of this would be over. He took a deep breath, rose and picked up the phone. Carefully he put it back on the nightstand, thanking God that his wife Teresa was at her mother's and wouldn't be back for a few more days. Plenty of time to get this taken care of before she returned.

As he headed for the door, he tried not to worry. Once Margaret Randolph was dead, no one would ever find out the truth. And it would never get back that he hadn't taken care of this problem twenty-seven years ago as he'd been paid to do.

One moment of kindness... He scoffed at his own worn lie. He'd done it for the money. Plain and simple. He'd sold the baby instead of disposing of it. And he'd never regretted it—until Paul Randolph found out the truth. Now Rupert had to take care of things quickly and efficiently before everything blew up in his face. No more mistakes like the one he'd made the other night at the pier. There was no way he should have missed her. He'd been too close and was too good of a shot.

He tried to put the mistakes behind him. Look to the future. And the future was simple. If Margaret Randolph wasn't floating in Puget Sound with the fish, she soon would be.

MAGGIE STARED at the sheriff's deputy uniform and tried to breathe. Jesse Tanner was a cop? Last night he'd said he knew the sheriff. She'd just assumed because it was a small town, everyone knew everyone else.

She stifled a groan. Not only had she stayed in the house of the local deputy, but now he might have the plate number on her bike. If he'd had reason to take it down.

Fear turned her blood to ice. He could find out her last name—if he didn't already know. Worse, he could tell Blackmore that not only was she alive but that she was in Timber Falls.

But why would Jesse Tanner run the plate number on her bike? She hadn't given him any reason to. Cops didn't need a reason though. And everyone knew they stuck together.

Except Jesse was different. He didn't act like a cop. Didn't insist she go to the doctor last night or the sheriff this morning. Didn't ask a lot of questions.

She tried to calm her pounding heart. Her hands were shaking as she wiped down the faucets and anything else she might have touched. Were her fingerprints on a file somewhere? She didn't know.

She thought she remembered being fingerprinted as a child. She knew her parents had worried about her being kidnapped. How ironic. And she'd always thought it was because of their wealth.

As she opened the bathroom door, she half expected the deputy to be waiting for her just outside. The hallway was empty. She stood listening.

Silence. Tiptoeing down the hall, she passed his open doorway again. He had rolled over, his back to her now. She prayed he would stay asleep as she eased into the screened-in deck where she'd slept.

She picked up her boots, her jacket and the saddlebag stuffed with most of the ten grand from the pier. Then she looked around to make sure she hadn't left anything behind before she limped quietly down the stairs.

At the bottom, she glanced at his paintings as she pulled on her boots, the left going on painfully because of her ankle. What she now knew about the man upstairs seemed at odds with his art. Jesse Tanner and his chisel-cut features, the deep set of matching dimples, the obsidian black eyes and hair, the ponytail and the gold earring didn't go with the deputy sheriff's uniform.

There was a wildness about the man, something he seemed to be trying to keep contained, but couldn't hide in his artwork. The large, bold strokes, the use of color, the way he portrayed his subjects.

Her favorite of the six paintings propped against the wall was a scene from a Mexican cantina. A series of men were watching a Latin woman dance. The sexual tension was like a coiled spring. In both the work and the painter.

He was talented, too talented not to be painting full-time. So why was he working as a sheriff's deputy? He didn't seem like the type who liked busting people for a living. Quite the opposite.

She glanced around the cabin. She liked it. Liked him. Wished he wasn't a cop. She told herself she shouldn't feel guilty for just running out on him.

Last night she'd been shaken from her accident, hurt and exhausted. She had needed a refuge and he'd provided it, asking nothing in return. He would never know how much that meant to her.

Under other circumstances, she would never have left without thanking him. But these were far from normal circumstances, she reminded herself and remembered the glass of whiskey she'd drunk last night.

Going to the sink, she turned on the faucet and washed both glasses thoroughly, then dried them. Being careful not to leave her prints anywhere, she set the glasses back on the cabinet shelf with the others and wiped down the faucet and handles just as she had in the bathroom upstairs.

She knew she was being overly cautious. But maybe that was why she was still alive.

Her bike was sitting outside, her helmet on the seat as if he'd put it there to let her know it was ready to go. He'd fixed the kickstand and straightened the twisted metal, as well as the handlebars. The bike was scraped up but didn't look too bad considering how close a call she'd had. Now if it would just run as well as it had.

She strapped on the saddlebag, then climbed on the bike, rolled it off the kickstand and turned the key.

The powerful motor rumbled to life and she felt a swell of relief—and appreciation for the man who'd fixed it. As she popped it into gear, she couldn't help herself. She glanced up at the house, then quickly looked away. He was a cop. She had learned the hard way not to trust them. Not to trust anyone. If she hoped to stay alive, she had to keep it that way.

JESSE TANNER stood at the screened window watching her leave. He'd been awakened by the sound of running water downstairs and had half hoped she was making coffee. He should have known better.

But he couldn't help worrying as he watched her ride off into the dawn. Last night after he'd finished with the bike, he'd looked in on her. He felt guilty for snooping but he'd looked into the heavy saddlebag and seen the bundles of money. Maybe she didn't believe in traveler's checks. Maybe she'd withdrawn all of her savings from the bank for a long bike trip. Or maybe she'd robbed a savings and loan.

Either way, she was gone and not his problem.

Nor should he be surprised she would leave like this without a word. Last night he'd gotten the impression she wasn't one for long goodbyes.

Still, he would have made her pancakes for breakfast if she'd hung around. Hell, he hadn't had pancakes in months, but he would have made them for her.

He went downstairs, foolishly hoping she'd left him

a note. He knew better. Her kind didn't leave notes. No happy faces on Post-Its on the fridge, no little heart dotting the *i* in her name. She was not that kind of girl.

He made a pot of coffee and saw that she'd washed their glasses and put them away. He stood for a long time just staring at the clean glasses as the coffee brewed, then he poured himself a cup and took it back upstairs while he showered and dressed in his uniform hanging on the back of the bathroom door, all the time dreading the day ahead.

It wasn't just the biker chick with the bag of money and worry over what she might be running from that had him bummed. She was miles away by now.

His problem was Desiree Dennison. He'd recognized the little red sports car that had sideswiped the biker last night. He couldn't turn a blind eye to what he'd seen: Desiree leaving the scene of an accident.

But the last thing he wanted to do was go out to the Dennisons and with good reason.

Chapter Four

Maggie cruised through Timber Falls in the early morning, surprised to find the town even smaller than the map had led her to believe. The main drag was only a few blocks long. Ho Hum Motel, Betty's Café, the Busy Bee antique shop, the Spit Curl, Harry's Hardware, a small post office, bank and auto body shop.

Past the *Cascade Courier* newspaper office she spotted the cop shop. She turned down a side street, avoiding driving by the sheriff's department even though she knew Jesse Tanner couldn't have beat her to town. But she had no way of knowing how many officers there were in this little burg, or who might be looking for her.

When she'd rolled off the pier, she'd taken Norman's body with her into the water. The surf was rough that night. As far as she knew Norman's body hadn't turned up yet, but then, she hadn't had a chance to check a newspaper. Until Norman's body was found, Blackmore might not be aware that she was still alive.

Last night she hadn't gone home. Fortunately, she'd been smart enough to hide her motorcycle before going down to the pier to meet Norman. When she'd crawled out of the water after being shot, she'd come up a hundred yards down the beach near a small seafood shack.

Keeping to the shadows, she'd broken in, stripped off her leathers down to the shorts and tank top she wore underneath and bandaged her arm as best she could with the first aid kit she found behind the counter.

Then she'd set off the fire alarm, hiding until the fire trucks arrived. In the commotion, she'd worked her way back to her bike, carrying her leathers in a garbage bag she'd taken from the café's kitchen.

She'd feared the cop would have found her bike and have it staked out but she didn't see anyone. Nor had she found any tracking devices on it when she'd checked later.

Running scared, she'd gone the only direction she could. Toward Timber Falls, Oregon, a tiny dot she'd found on a service station map. With luck, she'd bought herself a little time. Once Norman's body washed up and hers didn't, they were bound to get suspicious. Whoever they were.

Norman. Oh, Norman. She still felt sick and still blamed herself for his death. If she hadn't called Blackmore…

She'd called Rupert Blackmore because he was the detective investigating Clark Iverson's murder and she'd read in the paper that he was actively looking for the attorney's legal assistant, Norman Drake, for questioning. She knew nothing about the cop, let alone if he had a tie in with Timber Falls. Or her.

But she understood now why Norman was so freaked out. He had seen Detective Blackmore kill Iverson and, like Maggie, he had probably seen the recent photograph of Blackmore in the paper getting some award from the mayor for bravery and years of distinguished service in the Seattle Police Department.

Who would believe that a cop who'd been on the force for thirty years and received so many commendations was a killer? No one. That's why Norman hadn't gone to the cops. That's why Maggie knew she couldn't until she knew why Blackmore had murdered the others—and tried to kill her, as well.

Now she passed through a small residential area of town, coming out next to the Duck-In bar and Harper's Grocery. Her stomach growled and she tried to remember the last time she'd eaten and couldn't.

Parking beside the market in the empty lot, she went in and bought herself a bag of doughnuts and a carton of milk, downing most of the milk as she gathered supplies. She purchased some fruit and lunch-meat for later and a bottle of water. She wouldn't be back to town for hours.

As she started to check out she saw a rack of newspapers and braced herself. But before she could look for a story in one of the larger West Coast papers about a body floating up on a beach, she spotted a headline in the *Cascade Courier* that stopped her heart cold.

"HERE, YOU FORGOT THIS," Sheriff Mitch Tanner said from his recliner as Jesse walked through the door.

Jesse's first stop in town was to see how his brother was doing—and talk to him about the accident last night on the highway.

Mitch had always been the good one. College right after high school, then he'd taken the job as sheriff and bought a house. Mr. Law-Abiding.

Jesse on the other hand had been the wild older brother. Always in trouble. When he'd left Timber Falls it had been in handcuffs. After that little misunderstanding was cleared up, he'd headed for Mexico and had spent years down there, half-afraid to come home and yet missing his brother and dad.

"It's required that you have it with you at all times—and keep it turned *on,*" Mitch said, tossing him a cell phone.

Jesse groaned as he caught the damned thing. It was bad enough being a cop let alone having to carry a cell phone. He stuffed it into his pants pocket, telling himself it was only for a couple of months tops. "It's one of those that vibrates, right?" he asked with a wink. "Maybe it won't be so bad."

Mitch rolled his eyes and laid back in the recliner, his left leg in a huge cast and a pair of crutches leaning against the wall next to him. He'd taken two bullets, one had broken the tibia of his left leg. The other had just passed through his side. Both had laid him low though.

Worse, Mitch hadn't taken it well that his first bullet wound in uniform would be from someone he knew—the most famous man in Timber Falls, Wade Dennison. Wade had shot Mitch while struggling over a .38

with his estranged wife, Daisy. Mitch had just been in the wrong place at the wrong time.

Or at least that was Wade's story.

Jesse thought being behind bars was the perfect place for Wade. The man owned Dennison Ducks, the wooden decoy carving plant and pretty much the reason for the town's existence and because of that Wade Dennison had thrown his weight around for years.

Well, after being patched up at the hospital he was now behind bars facing all kinds of charges, including assault with a deadly weapon, resisting arrest and domestic abuse. His wife Daisy was fighting for no bail, saying she feared for her life should Wade be released.

Needless to say, it made great headlines in the *Cascade Courier*, the weekly local paper run by Mitch's fiancée Charity Jenkins. In fact, Charity seemed to be doing everything she could to keep the story page one.

And, as always, the news kept the gossips going at Betty's Café.

Jesse knew a lot of people in town resented Wade because of his money and his overbearing attitude and were hoping when the trial rolled around that Wade got the book thrown at him. Jesse just hoped Wade never went gunning for Mitch again. He would definitely take it personally next time.

Meanwhile, since Mitch was off his feet, he'd asked Jesse to stand in as acting deputy until he was completely recovered. Jesse had helped him out before since his return to Timber Falls. Because the town was in a remote part of Oregon, the sheriff had the authority to deputize whatever help he needed.

Jesse suspected Mitch thought putting him in a uniform would help straighten him up. He smiled at the thought because the job was a mixed blessing. He had only started this morning and already hated it. Still, he figured he was doing Mitch a favor and he could use the money, but he'd never been wild about cops since his wild youth and now he was one. The only one in Timber Falls.

The good news was that Timber Falls seldom had any real crime. Although this rainy season had had more than its share. But Jesse was hoping that with Wade Dennison locked up in jail and no more bigfoot sightings, things would quiet down.

"You look like you're doing all right," he said to his brother as Charity came into the room with a tray of coffee, freshly squeezed orange juice, scrambled eggs, bacon and toast. She put it down on Mitch's lap.

Jesse raised a brow. "Damn, the woman can even cook?"

"Very funny," Charity quipped. "It's genetic. All women are born to cook and clean. Men are born to be asses."

Jesse faked a hurt expression.

"Except for Mitch," she added with a smile as she touched his shoulder. Charity had been crazy about Jesse's younger brother since she was a kid and he couldn't be more excited that the two of them were finally getting married. Mitch, while lying in a pool of his own blood, finally got smart and proposed to her after she'd helped save his life. The man was slow, but not stupid.

"I need to talk to my little brother for a moment," Jesse said. Mitch was two years younger, but several inches taller than Jesse. "Sheriff's department business."

Mitch groaned. "That's like waving a red flag in front of a bull to talk sheriff's department business in front of Charity, ace reporter."

"It's nothing you'd find interesting for the newspaper," Jesse assured Charity as he sat down next to Mitch and stole a piece of his bacon. Charity stuck around just in case. She was the owner, editor and reporter of the *Cascade Courier* and she was a bloodhound when it came to a good story.

"You know those forms you said I have to file every week?" Jesse said chewing the bacon. "Where again do you keep them?"

Charity picked up her purse and headed for the front door. "Jesse, if you're going to be here for a few minutes, I need to run by the paper."

"I *can* be left alone, you know," Mitch called to her. "I'm not a complete invalid."

Charity paid him no mind.

"I'll stay here until you come back," Jesse proposed so she would finally leave.

"Forms?" Mitch said after she'd gone.

Jesse shrugged. "Couldn't think of anything else off the top of my head. The real reason I wanted to talk to you is that I witnessed an accident last night. Desiree Dennison ran a biker off the road."

Mitch swore. "Anyone hurt?"

Jesse shook his head. "It was a hit-and-run though. She didn't even stop to see if the biker was okay."

"You're sure it was Desiree?"

"Saw the car with my own eyes. She had the top

down. No one has a head of hair like her.'' Desiree took great pride in that wild mane of hers.

He was trying to put his finger on just what color it was when he was reminded of the biker's hair. It was long and fell in soft curls down her back and was a dark mahogany color that only nature could create. Desiree's was darker than he remembered and he realized she must have put something on it.

''Any other witnesses?'' Mitch asked.

''Not at 3:00 a.m.''

''What about the biker?''

''Wasn't interested in pressing charges. You know bikers.''

Mitch grunted. He knew Jesse and that was enough.

''There's going to be damage to the car. The biker hit the passenger door side. I'd say pretty extensive damage and I took a sample of the paint from the bike.''

Mitch was nodding. ''You have to write Desiree up. The judge is going to take her license, has to after all her speeding tickets.''

Jesse nodded. ''I just wanted to tell you before I go up there. I'm sure there will be repercussions.''

Mitch snorted. ''With a Dennison?''

''I heard Wade might make bail.''

''No way. Daisy's fighting it. So am I. He's too much of a risk.''

''I hope the judge sees it that way,'' Jesse said as he took a piece of Mitch's toast. He'd never had much faith in the system. And Charity had been writing some pretty inflammatory news articles about Wade and the rest of the Dennisons, dragging up a lot of old dirt.

If Wade got out, who knew what he would do. He'd threatened to kill Charity at least once that Jesse knew of.

"Have you considered cutting your hair?" Mitch asked eyeing him as Jesse wiped his bacon-greasy hands on his brother's napkin.

"Nope." That was the good part about being deputized in this part of Oregon. A lot of the rules in the big city just didn't apply. How else could someone like Jesse become an officer of the law?

He heard Charity's VW pull up. "Your woman's back. Better eat your breakfast."

"What's left of it," Mitch grumbled. "Be careful up there at the Dennisons'. I swear they're all crazy."

Jesse wouldn't argue that.

MAGGIE STARED at the newspaper headline. After Twenty-Seven Years In Hiding Following Daughter's Kidnapping, Daisy Dennison Ready For New Life.

"Is that all?" the grocery clerk asked.

Maggie dragged her gaze away from the newspaper to look at the older woman behind the counter. Twenty-seven years. Kidnapping. "What?"

"Is there anything else?"

"I'll take a few papers," Maggie said, feeling lightheaded and nauseous as she grabbed the two larger West Coast papers and one of the tiny *Cascade Courier*. She shoved them into the grocery bag with her other purchases, her hands shaking.

The clerk eyed her for a moment, then rang up the

newspapers. Maggie gave her a twenty and accepted the change the woman insisted on counting out into her trembling palm. Stuffing the change into the bag with the groceries, Maggie left, trying not to run.

Outside she gulped the damp morning air as she scanned the streets, not sure if she was looking for the face of a killer, that of a handsome dimpled sheriff's deputy or maybe a face that resembled her own.

The streets were empty at this early hour. She looked back to find the clerk still watching her.

Climbing onto her bike, Maggie backtracked a few blocks to make sure no one was following her, then rode south out of town to one of the dozens of state campgrounds she'd seen on the map. She picked a closed one, wound her way around the barrier until she found a campsite farthest from the highway, deep in the woods and near the river.

It wasn't until she was pretty sure she was safe that she dragged out the newspapers, starting with the article in the *Cascade Courier*.

She read it in its entirety twice. There was little about the original kidnapping. Mostly it was a story about a woman named Daisy Dennison who had been a recluse for twenty-seven years after her baby daughter had been stolen from her crib.

Her husband Wade, the founder of Dennison Ducks, a local decoy carving plant, was behind bars for a variety of things including shooting the sheriff during a recent domestic dispute with Daisy.

Wade Dennison's attempts to make bail had been thwarted by his wife. Daisy, it was alleged, had filed for divorce and had started a new life.

What a great family, Maggie thought sarcastically.

But what Maggie did get from the story was that the couple's youngest daughter, Angela, had been kidnapped twenty-seven years ago. No ransom had ever been demanded. Angela was never seen again.

Angela Dennison. Was it possible Maggie was this person? If what Norman had told her was correct, she had to be. How many other babies had been kidnapped from this tiny town twenty-seven years ago?

She quickly set up her two-man tent and finished off the milk and a couple more doughnuts before going through the larger newspapers. Nothing about Norman. She breathed a sigh of relief.

She knew she should try to get some sleep but the river pooled just through the trees near her campsite, clear and welcoming. She left the tent and walked over to the small pool, stripped down and took a bath. The icy cold water did more than clean and refresh her. It assured her she was alive. At least for the time being.

Full and feeling better, she still felt restless, anxious for the cloak of darkness so she could return to town—and worried about the deputy she'd stayed with part of the night. He had no reason to come looking for her. Unless he'd been warned she might be headed to Timber Falls. But then, that would mean Jesse Tanner had been in contact with Detective Rupert Blackmore and Blackmore knew she was alive.

Would the deputy help Blackmore find her? Why wouldn't he? It would be her word against a respected detective. No contest.

She hid her bike in the trees, then brought the saddlebag full of money and her meager toiletries and clothing into the tent to wait until dark.

Chapter Five

Jesse had made a point of steering clear of the Dennisons since the time he was a boy. The last thing he wanted to do was ruin the morning by confronting Desiree, let alone her mother Daisy.

But he stopped by the sheriff's department just long enough to leave his Harley and pick up the patrol car Mitch insisted he use along with that damned cell phone.

The Dennisons lived a few miles outside of town not far from Dennison Ducks.

Jesse hadn't seen Wade and Daisy's daughter Desiree since the shooting at the Dennison house when his brother had been wounded.

But he'd heard Desiree had been frequenting the Duck-In Bar more than usual and driving like a bat out of hell in that cute little sports car Daddy had bought her before he went to jail.

The last time he was at the house he'd found them all in the pool house, Mitch lying on the floor bleeding and Daisy with the gun trying to kill Wade. Fun family. Charity had saved the day—and Mitch—and all

Jesse had needed to do was handcuff Wade and haul him off to the hospital then jail, adding to the scandal that had been a part of that family from as far back as Jesse could remember. Long before their youngest daughter had been kidnapped twenty-seven years before.

Needless to say, neither Daisy nor Desiree was going to be anxious to see him again. The feeling was mutual.

He parked his patrol car near the four-car garage and climbed out, the Dennison mansion looming out of the forest in front of him.

The place had been built with one thing in mind, letting everyone know just how much money Wade had and how much more could be made through duck decoys. It was an overdone plantation house straight out of *Gone With the Wind.* Antebellum style with huge pillars, a massive veranda complete with white wicker and inside, a Timber Falls' version of southern belles. Except Daisy, like her daughter Desiree, was no Southerner. Nor was either a belle.

He checked the garage first, peeking in the windows. There was Wade's SUV. Daisy's SUV. And Desiree's little red sports car, the passenger side caved in. He opened the garage door and stepped in, taking the chip of paint he'd scraped from the bike out of his pocket and holding it up against the car door panel. Perfect match. As if there had ever been any doubt. Then he headed for the main house.

"Would you please get Miss Desiree up, ma'am," he said in his best Rhett Butler imitation when the housekeeper answered the front door of the house a few minutes later. ''It's the law come a calling.'' He flashed his credentials.

The German housekeeper didn't get the accent or the humor, what little there was. Nor did she look the least bit concerned. It wasn't as if this was the first time a uniformed officer had come to the door looking for Desiree.

''She is indisposed.''

Jesse laughed. ''She's still in bed. If I have to come back it will be with a warrant for her arrest.''

''I'll take care of this,'' said a female voice from the cool darkness of the house. Daisy stepped from the shadows. She was close to fifty and still a very attractive woman. It seemed as if the years she'd spent in seclusion after Angela's kidnapping had made her more reserved, less haughty. Her dark hair had been recently highlighted with blond streaks and cut to the nape of her neck so that it floated nicely around her pretty face.

But Jesse would always see her as he had at the age of nine, a goddess with long dark hair and a lush body, riding bareback through the tall grass behind his house, smelling of fancy flowers and what he later realized was sex.

''Hello, Jesse. Can I offer you some coffee? Or perhaps a glass of iced tea? Zinnia just made some.''

''No, thank you, Mrs. Dennison.'' He supposed it was natural he was disposed not to like the woman even if he had never spoken more than two words to her before. ''I need to see Desiree.''

''I'm sure she's still in bed. Please. Call me Daisy.''

"I'm going to have to insist you get her up, Mrs. Dennison."

Daisy's back stiffened. So did her features. "It's that important?"

"Yes, ma'am, it is."

She sighed. "Very well. If you'd care to wait in there." She pointed toward a small sitting room, the walls lined with books. "I'll go get her." Her look said Desiree would not be happy about this.

Too bad. He was a hell of a lot less happy about this than the princess of the house.

It was a good forty-five minutes later before Desiree made an appearance. Jesse had reacquainted himself with several classics in the small library by the time she burst into the room.

Her scent preceded her. She smelled of jasmine, her hair still wet from her shower, her face perfectly made-up. She was wearing all white, a blouse that floated over her curves and white Capri pants that set off her sun-bed tanned legs. She gave him her come-hither look, but being seductive came as easily as breathing for Desiree.

"Jesse," she cooed. "You really should call a girl before you drop by so she can be presentable."

He was struck by the color of her eyes. But it wasn't just the eyes, he realized.

She moved past him, darting to plant a kiss on his cheek and brushing one of her full breasts against his arm as she did.

He found his voice. "This is not a social occasion and you know it."

She turned to smile at him. Desiree Dennison had

found that she possessed a power over men and she loved it.

"I'm here on sheriff's department business," he said. "I witnessed an accident last night on the highway by my place. I saw you hit a motorcyclist when you pulled out from Maple Creek Road."

She drew back, gave him a get-real look, then lied right to his face. "I don't know what you're talking about."

"Where were you at three in the morning, after the bars closed?"

A brow shot up. "In bed."

"Anyone's bed I know who can give you an alibi?"

She pouted. "In my own bed, alone."

He shook his head. "Give me your car keys."

"What?"

"Your car keys. Now."

"I'll have to go upstairs and get them." Her cheeks flamed with obvious anger as if the walk was more than she was up to this morning. Or maybe it was being caught.

"I'll wait."

She turned her back on him to buzz the housekeeper on the intercom. "Get me some juice," she snapped. "Orange juice. A large glass." Then she left the room.

He half expected to hear the sports car engine roar to life, but Desiree was too used to getting out of scrapes to make a run for it. Daddy always bailed her out. Only Daddy couldn't even make bail himself right now. And maybe Mommy was over Desiree's shenanigans.

But it was Daisy who returned with the car keys.

"If you had told me why you were here, I could have saved you the trouble of waking Desiree. I was driving my daughter's car last night."

He stared at her, not bothering to take the keys she held out to him. "You were the one up Maple Creek Road? You realize that's the local make-out spot?"

She smiled. "Is it? I'm afraid I was only turning around. I took Desiree's car because I felt like having the top down. I pulled into the turnoff at Maple Creek Road. I didn't see the biker. I know I should have reported it at once."

"Or maybe stopped to see if the biker wasn't killed."

Daisy blanched. "Is he all right?"

Jesse didn't correct her on the rider's gender. "Yeah."

Her expression said she expected charges to be filed, probably a lawsuit by the biker, maybe even her own arrest, but she was ready. Like her daughter, she'd always come away from scrapes unscathed. Except for the loss of her youngest daughter, Angela, when Desiree was two.

"Are you surc you want to take the rap for your daughter?" Jesse asked, holding her gaze. "I know Desiree was driving the car. I saw her."

"Really? You were making out on Maple Creek Road last night, deputy?" Daisy asked.

He smiled. "No, I was standing on the deck of my cabin. I can see the highway from there."

"From your house?" Daisy repeated. "From that distance and in the dark you are absolutely sure it was Desiree behind the wheel?"

"Yes."

"How is that possible when I was the one driving her car?" Daisy asked.

He knew exactly what she was saying. He could call her a liar and press this. It would be his word against hers. He might be wearing a deputy's uniform but she would be more credible—even after the shoot-out in her pool house. Maybe more so because she had come off as the victim. Plus she would hire the best attorney money could buy.

"Look, the worst that will happen is Desiree will lose her driver's license," he said patiently. "And you know that's probably the best thing that could happen, getting her off the streets for a while. Next time she might kill someone. Or herself. And there *will* be a next time."

"I told you I was the one—"

"I know what you told me," Jesse interrupted. "You also told me that Wade was the one who shot my brother but it was your gun and your hand over Wade's when the shots were fired."

Daisy's gaze turned to granite. "I'm sorry about Mitch. I was only trying to defend myself."

Or make sure Wade was out of her life—and without the money, the house, the business. Jesse fought to hold his temper in check. "Isn't that the same thing Wade said when he killed Bud Farnsworth?"

She flinched imperceptibly. The former production manager at Dennison Ducks had pretty much confessed to kidnapping baby Angela from her crib twenty-seven years ago. Unfortunately, Bud never had the chance to implicate the person believed to have masterminded the kidnapping—or tell anyone what he'd done with Angela.

According to Charity, who'd been there, Bud had been trying to say something when Wade shot and killed him. Wade's defense was that he was protecting Charity and Daisy.

"In two months time, you've been involved in two shootings," Jesse pointed out.

"I was shot myself by Mr. Farnsworth, you might recall," Daisy said. "And almost killed by my estranged husband. In my emotional state is it any wonder I didn't see that motorcycle last night let alone that I panicked and foolishly didn't stop?"

He had to laugh. She would play whatever card it took to get herself out of this—and damned if she wouldn't walk.

"Are you going to arrest me?" she asked. "If so I'd like to call my lawyer."

"You can call your lawyer from the sheriff's office," Jesse said. "Sure you don't want to rethink what you're doing, Mrs. Dennison?"

She hesitated but only for a moment, then held out her wrists to be handcuffed.

It was a temptation. "I don't think that will be necessary as long as you promise to come along without any trouble."

She smiled and walked to the intercom. "I'll be back shortly, Desiree."

Desiree didn't come back downstairs. Not even when Zinnia showed up with a large glass of freshly squeezed orange juice.

CHARITY CHECKED to make sure Mitch had fallen asleep before she let Aunt Florie in the front door and took her aside.

"Don't try to force anything with tofu in it on him, all right?" Charity whispered so as to not disturb Mitch who was snoring softly in his recliner. "Or zucchini."

"He likes my zucchini bread," Florie said.

Sure Mitch did. If Charity hadn't been desperate, she would never have even considered leaving Florie with Mitch, but Wade Dennison's sister, Lydia Abernathy, had asked her to stop by the antique shop. Charity was dying to know what that was about. Wade and his recent arrest probably. Charity had always suspected Lydia knew a lot more about what went on at her brother's house than she was telling.

"And no reading his palm or his tea leaves, got it?" Mitch wouldn't be happy to wake up to Florie. But Charity's aunt and all her other screwball relatives came with the marriage package. No wonder Mitch had taken so long to pop the question.

"Whatever." Florie smiled. She'd been doing that a lot lately. Ever since Liam Sawyer had become single again. "Just a minute. I don't know what to wear to the party this weekend." She whipped two caftans out of her bag, one in swirls of bright colors, the other in splashes of bright colors. "Which do you like best?"

That was a tough one. They were both garish at best. "I have an idea," Charity said looking at her aunt. "I think it's time for a makeover."

Florie, now hugging seventy, was the local psychic

and ran her business, Madam Florie's, via e-mail from an old motel on the south end of town. The motel units were now bungalow rentals and Florie did readings out of the office-slash-apartment, as well as on the Internet.

Whether or not Florie was clairvoyant was debatable. But she definitely played the part. She wore her long dyed red hair wound around her head like a turban, and dressed in bright caftans that mirrored the turquoise eye shadow she wore to highlight her blue eyes. Her fingers were adorned with dozens of rings and her slim wrists jangled with an array of colorful bracelets. She looked like an exotic bird, blinding in its plumage.

"What's wrong with the way I look?" Florie asked.

Charity didn't have enough time to get into that. "I just think maybe Roz and I could give you a new look for the party." Roz was Liam Sawyer's daughter. The party was to celebrate the fact that her best friend Rozalyn was back in town to stay. Also, Charity suspected, to announce Roz's engagement to Ford Lancaster.

"A new look?" Florie repeated.

Charity nodded enthusiastically. "A surprise for Liam."

The older woman's eyes brightened and Charity knew she had her. Florie had been in love with Liam for years.

"I'll talk to Roz. Don't you worry. It's going to be great," Charity whispered, backing toward the door. "I'll be back as soon as I can. Don't forget, nothing funny on Mitch."

Florie had that dreamy look on her face, obviously lost in thought about Liam, as she waved from the front porch.

Charity had to smile as she climbed into her VW Bug. It was nice to know that falling in love had no age limit. She hoped things worked out for her aunt and Liam. Meanwhile, she couldn't wait to find out what Lydia Abernathy wanted. Lydia only called when something was up.

AFTER LOCKING UP Daisy Dennison, Jesse drove through town, fighting a bad mood, hoping to see that fancy motorbike he'd rolled into the back of his pickup last night.

He couldn't get Maggie—if that was her real name—off his mind. Or the money he'd seen in her saddlebag. But there was no sign of her.

Back at the office, he whizzed past Sissy, taking the handful of messages she waved at him, as he went by. Sissy, a thirtysomething large woman with an attitude, managed to get in one of her your-name-is-mud looks before he closed the door.

He sat down behind his brother's desk, glaring at the computer. After a moment, he looked through the messages. Barking dog, missing trash can, abandoned car, noise complaint. He recognized the names of the people who had called. Constant complainers. All people his brother had to deal with on a daily basis—especially this time of year when the constant rain caused a bad case of cabin fever. Jesse wondered how Mitch did it.

Dropping the messages on his desk, he stared at the

computer. He'd written down the license number from Maggie's bike last night when he'd hoped she would press charges. Now he hesitated.

"Sissy?" he said buzzing the clerk.

"Yeesss?"

He cringed, only desperation would make him call her in here, but he was about as wild about computers as he was cell phones. "I need help."

That soft knowing chuckle of hers. "Don't I know it."

A minute later she opened the office door and stepped in, hands on hips. "If you want coffee, you get it yourself. Doughnuts, I get 'em every morning anyway so I don't mind picking up a couple for the sheriff. He liked lemon-filled."

"Lemon-filled works for me," Jesse said.

"And it would help if you told me where you were going when you left. Better yet," she said, swinging her head to one side with obvious attitude, "if you bothered to show up in the morning at all. People call wanting to know there is someone in charge and what am I supposed to tell them?"

"I thought *you* were in charge," he said and smiled.

She mugged a face at him. "You better believe it."

He reminded himself that he only had to do this for a couple of months tops and if he could deal with Daisy and Desiree Dennison he could put up with Sissy Walker. As long as he didn't spend too much time in the office.

"You know how to run this damned thing?" he said, motioning to the computer.

She smiled that smug smile of hers. ''The Pope wear boxers?''

He didn't have a clue. But she hadn't moved. ''Can you *show* me how to use it?'' She still didn't move. ''Please? Pretty please and I buy the doughnuts?''

A smile burst across her ample face and she sashayed over, shooed him up and planted her wide hips in his chair. ''What you want?''

''Show me how to find out things. Like...how do I track down a name from a license plate number?''

''What state?''

''Washington. A motorcycle license.''

She kicked up an eyebrow and gave him a look but began to tap the keys. He paid attention. He might not like computers, but he was a fast learner and he wasn't going to call in Sissy every time he needed to look up a plate number.

''What's the number?''

He told her, then watched the screen anxiously to see what she came up with.

Sissy let out an ''uh-huh,'' as the name appeared on the screen. ''I should have known it would be some broad.''

''Biker chick,'' he corrected, reading the name Margaret Jane Randolph—Maggie—and the address, a better-known wealthy residential area in West Seattle. He hadn't expected anything less.

Sissy started to get up.

''Wait, one more thing. How would I see if there are any priors on her?''

Sissy gave him that eyebrow thing again but continued typing. "You know how to pick 'em," she said as an APB came up for the woman in question.

Margaret Jane Randolph was wanted for questioning in a murder investigation in West Seattle. Murder? The photo accompanying the APB looked as if it was her mug shot from her driver's license. Her hair was different but she was obviously the woman he'd picked up off the highway last night. No two women had a face like that even if some of her features might remind him of another woman.

He swore softly under his breath.

"Anything else?" Sissy asked sounding disgusted as she pushed herself up and started toward the door.

"No. Thanks," he said as he lowered himself into the chair she'd vacated.

Sissy stopped in the doorway. He glanced up at her. She was shaking her head, giving him the once-over, her gaze halting on his ponytail for a moment.

"How do I make a printout?" he called after her.

"Press Print. Some deputy you make," she said under her breath as she left the room, closing the door behind her.

He turned back to the screen.

An instant message box had flashed up, advising any inquiries to be routed to Detective Rupert Blackmore of the West Seattle Police Department. The message was marked urgent and included the detective's phone number.

Jesse stared at the message and swore. What the hell? It seemed pretty clear Maggie wasn't just wanted for questioning. Was it possible she was a suspect in the murder investigation? And where did all the cash fit in? Or did it?

Jesse got up and walked to the window, telling himself there was no reason to call the detective. No reason to pursue this. She was long gone. Hell, she could be halfway to Mexico by now. Or at least California.

Outside, it had started to rain again, another gray day. Nothing new there.

The woman was wanted for questioning in a murder investigation? Damn.

He went back to the computer, jotted down the detective's name and number on a piece of scrap paper.

Then he hit the close key.

It took a long moment for the screen to clear and as he watched it, he wondered if Detective Rupert Blackmore was at this very moment wondering why someone at the sheriff's department in Timber Falls, Oregon, was interested in Maggie Randolph.

Chapter Six

Detective Rupert Blackmore left the crime scene trying not to panic. Margaret Randolph's body hadn't floated up and now he knew it wouldn't.

Williams had informed him that a fire alarm had been set off at a café a quarter mile downstream. A false alarm. Not just that, the owner of the café had told Williams that the place had been broken into, there were drops of blood on the floor and someone had used the first aid kit kept behind the counter.

After Rupert had shot them both, he'd waited in the fog for the bodies to float ashore. Waited until he heard the fire trucks and saw the flashing lights a quarter mile down the water at some wharfside café. He hadn't put it together then because he'd been so sure they were dead.

Hell, she'd gone down with the geek and she'd been hit. Even if the bullets hadn't killed her, the fall and the cold churning water would have, his mind argued. But the fog had been too damned thick to tell if she'd surfaced.

He reminded himself that she'd had on all leather.

It would have acted like a wetsuit. And the woman was an athlete.

Rupert knew it was time to quit lying to himself. Margaret Randolph's body wasn't going to float up. Worse, he couldn't forget those last few moments on the pier when she'd looked up at him. *Recognized* him.

He sat down at his desk and began to fish around in the top drawer for some Tums. His stomach was killing him.

He'd made the mistake of keeping an eye on her over the years. It was crazy, but he felt like she was his kid. Like he'd been the one to give her life. Hell, he had. If he'd done what he'd been paid to do, she would have died as a baby and been buried up in the mountains.

Is that why he'd blown it at the pier?

But if she was alive, then why hadn't she contacted his superiors? Or the Feds? If she was alive, wouldn't she tell someone what she knew?

Out of the corner of his eye he caught the flashing icon on his computer screen. His gaze jerked to it and he felt his heart take off like a thief.

He shot a quick glance behind him and saw that Williams was on the phone with someone and paying no attention. Hands shaking, he clicked on the icon and tried to catch his breath.

As the inquiry came up, his chest ached as if he'd been shot and for a moment he couldn't think, couldn't breathe. Funny, but he didn't even mind the thought of falling over dead at his desk. At least he didn't mind for those first few seconds. A heart attack seemed a better way out than any of the other alternatives right now.

But then he caught his breath, regained his senses, felt that primal survival instinct kick in. He wasn't ready to go out feet first. Hell, if he could weather this storm, he would retire like Teresa had been trying to get him to do. And he'd buy that damned RV she had her heart set on and the two of them would head south. No more rainy winters in the Northwest. They'd go to Arizona and he'd sit in the sun by the pool. Hell, yes. Maybe he'd take up shuffleboard or bingo. Why not?

He deleted the information on the screen, grabbed his coat and left the police station, driving around aimlessly, trying to think.

He'd tagged inquiries about Margaret Randolph only so he'd know firsthand when any evidence surfaced. He'd never dreamed he'd get a hit from some hick sheriff's department. And in Timber Falls, Oregon, of all places. Margaret Randolph's motorcycle tags had been run along with a check for any outstanding warrants on her. What the hell? Did that mean what he feared it did?

He tried to convince himself that someone else had her bike. Maybe had stolen it since he hadn't been able to find the bike after he'd seen her go off the end of the pier and into the icy, churning water below. She'd been wearing her biker outfit so he'd known she'd come by bike. He'd looked for it but was forced to leave for fear of being seen by emergency personnel. Her bike must have been hidden.

So where the hell was it now?

In Timber Falls, Oregon.

And how had it gotten there?

If Margaret Randolph had been riding it then… Hell, then she knew. Norman Drake must have overheard more than Rupert thought he did. Damn. If only he'd gotten to Norman Drake sooner. If only…

He pulled the car over, his hands still shaking, and waited for his heart rate to return to normal, knowing it wouldn't until he found her and finished the job.

Maybe her bike had been stolen though. Maybe her body *would* wash up.

His cell phone rang as if on cue. He fumbled it open, his pulse a deafening pounding in his ears. "Blackmore."

"It's Williams. The boys are done. It's raining and they haven't found anything else. You want me to leave a man down there? I'm not sure what else you were hoping we would find."

Another damned body. But then he couldn't very well tell Williams that, could he? "Tell them to pack it in. Listen, I'm not feeling very well."

"Ulcers again?"

"Goes with the job," he said. "I'm thinking I might take a day or two of sick pay. If there's anything new on the Iverson and Drake homicides just call me on my cell."

"Hope you get to feeling better," Williams said, but Rupert could hear his relief. The fool thought he could solve both cases and make a name for himself with the guys upstairs in the next forty-eight hours.

Down the block Rupert spotted a phone booth. He didn't want to use the company cell for this call. He parked, got out and ran through the pouring rain. He was soaked to the skin and breathing hard from the exertion by the time he ducked inside the booth. He promised himself he'd get in shape once he got to Arizona.

He dug out a handful of coins from his pocket, dialed the long-distance number and listened to it ring twice as he lit a cigarette and tried to calm down.

"Hello."

Teresa's voice brought tears to his eyes. He wiped at them with the back of his hand. "Hey, baby," he said, his voice breaking. "I was hoping I'd catch you."

"Is everything all right?" He could hear the worry in her tone. She knew him too well. But she didn't know the half of it. And he would die before he'd let her find out.

"I've got to go out of town for a couple of days on a case," he said. "I just wanted to let you know so you wouldn't worry about me if you called the house. How's your mom?"

"Better. She says to tell her favorite son-in-law hello."

It was an old joke between the three of them. "If I see him, I will."

Teresa laughed as she always did. "I miss you."

"Me, too." He could feel himself getting choked up again. He wished they'd had kids. Wished to hell he'd retired last year. Wished they were in Arizona right now.

But even as he thought it, he knew this wasn't something he could have avoided. Not even in Arizona.

"I'll call you when I finish this job," he said. "I've got to go."

"You take care of yourself, you hear?" It was what she always said.

"For you," he answered as he always did. He started to tell her he'd decided to retire. That they would buy that RV she liked as soon as she got back from her mother's so it would be all ready for them to go south at the first drop of rain next fall, but she'd already hung up.

As he put the receiver back and stood staring out through the soiled glass at the driving rain, Rupert realized what else had been bothering him.

The officer in Timber Falls who'd made the inquiry about Margaret Randolph hadn't called him. Why, when the hick cop had to have seen the message that he was to notify Detective Rupert Blackmore immediately?

He swore under his breath. He was sweating profusely even with the rain hammering the phone booth and a cold wet wind blowing up under the door.

He wasn't spending his golden years behind bars with criminals he'd put there. But he doubted that was even an option. If the person who'd hired him all those years ago found out who Margaret Randolph really was, then it would be clear that he hadn't killed her twenty-seven years ago. That he'd sold her instead and pocketed the cash. And then he'd be a dead man.

He watched the rain drum the glass of the phone booth without even hearing it or feeling the cold or the damp. After a few minutes, he started to breathe a little easier. He felt better. There was nothing like a plan.

He was going to Timber Falls. He'd put an end to this mess once and for all.

Pushing open the phone-booth door, he took a deep breath of the damp Seattle air and thought about Arizona.

Hell, by this time next year he could have a tan.

JESSE HAD JUST LOOKED UP from the computer when he caught a flash of color streak by on the street beyond his window. For just an instant, he thought it might be Maggie Randolph on that bike of hers.

But as he peered out the window, he saw it was Desiree's bright red sports car.

"I'll be a son of a—" He ran outside just as Desiree swung the car into Betty's Café and came to a dust-whirling stop.

He swore again and went after her.

Desiree was already sitting in a booth when Jesse walked in. She groaned when she saw him coming toward her. At least she knew she was in trouble. That was a start. He went straight to her booth and slid in across from her.

For a long moment, he just looked at her. She really was a pretty young woman, great bones, nice eyes. There was no denying that. But Desiree lacked something that the woman he'd met last night had in spades. Something beyond looks that had made her impossible to forget.

"What?" Desiree asked peevishly.

"I know your mother took the blame for you this

morning,'' he said quietly. She started to argue but he held up his hand. ''You don't learn. I just saw you speeding down Main Street. You're going to kill someone. Or yourself.''

''Are you going to write me a ticket?'' she asked, as if bored with this particular lecture.

''Desiree...''

She smiled and leaned toward him. ''Yes?''

''Get a job. Do something with your life before it's too late.'' He couldn't believe those words had come out of his mouth.

Neither could she. ''Jesse Tanner telling *me* to do something with *my* life?''

He smiled then and shook his head. ''I know I'm the last person who should be giving career advice sincc I'm just starting to get my act together and you're six years younger than me.''

''No kidding.''

He tried another tack. ''Is this about your father? Some sort of rebellion? Because if it is, I can relate.''

Her eyes narrowed at him in warning. ''Your father isn't in jail.''

''No, but I spent a few nights there as a juvenile and I can see a cell in your future if you don't stop acting out.''

She rolled her eyes.

''I'm trying to cut you some slack here,'' he said.

''Don't.''

''Okay.'' He pulled out his ticket book and wrote her up for speeding. He handed the ticket across the table to her as Desiree's lunch arrived.

She stuffed the ticket into her purse without looking

at it, picked up a piece of bacon that had fallen out of her BLT and took a bite, licking her lips as her gaze met his. "You want a bite?"

"No."

"Sure?" She cranked up the seduction, obviously in her comfort zone again.

He got to his feet. He'd hoped maybe he could talk some sense into her. Or at least reach out to her in a brotherly sort of way. He felt like he owed her that for reasons he didn't want to touch.

As he left, he felt it again—something in the air. The way he could sense a storm coming. As if the atmosphere were electrically charged. He stopped to sniff the breeze, unable to shake the bad feeling he had. It was as if something was about to happen and nothing could stop it. Least of all Acting Deputy Jesse Tanner.

"CHARITY, PUNCTUAL AS ALWAYS," Lydia Abernathy called from the back as Charity walked through the door of the Busy Bee antique shop a few minutes later.

Lydia smiled and waved from her wheelchair. She was a tiny woman, her hair a white downy halo around her head, her blue eyes bright. She looked older than Charity knew her to be. No doubt because of the accident that had severed her spinal cord and killed her beloved husband, Henry.

It had happened thirty years ago, before Charity was born, but she remembered Florie telling her that Wade had been driving the car. Henry had died instantly, Lydia had ended up in a wheelchair and Wade had gotten off without a scratch.

It was no secret that Wade felt responsible. He'd taken care of his sister for years, supporting her financially, opening the antique shop she'd always wanted and making sure she had live-in help.

They were close in spite of the past. Although Lydia, like most siblings, did take perverse pleasure in her brother's troubles. And Wade had his share right now.

"I heard about your upcoming nuptials," Lydia said as she moved her wheelchair over to the hot plate to collect the teapot. "I thought we'd celebrate with a cup of tea and a few of my sugar cookies."

"You know I can't resist your sugar cookies," Charity said with a groan. "The ones with the sprinkles on top?"

Lydia beamed. "Of course. Angus insists I do too much. He says he's taking over the baking."

Angus Smythe was Timber Falls' version of an English butler. Silent unless spoken to, always painfully polite, and very protective and attentive of Lydia. Plus, he was from England and came complete with the accent. He'd been a close friend of both Lydia and Henry. He was obviously devoted to her.

Charity dragged up a chair, glancing around the shop. The merchandise hardly ever changed. Lydia had collected pieces via the Internet but had marked them up so much they weren't likely to sell. Charity suspected she just liked having pretty things around and wasn't in the antique business to make money. Fortunately, she didn't have to show a profit. She had her brother Wade when she needed money.

"So when is the wedding?" Lydia asked, handing

her a cup of tea, a sugar cookie lounging on the saucer next to it.

Charity knew this wasn't why Lydia had asked to see her. "June. Everyone in town will be invited. I'm just starting the planning."

The older woman nodded. "Henry and I had a lovely wedding." Her eyes clouded over for a moment as if lost in memory. "Henry's buried back East, you know, in the family plot. I will join him when the time comes. I only stayed out here to be close to Wade." She grimaced. "Can you believe the mess he has himself in now? And all because he married beneath his class."

Lydia took a sip of her tea and settled the cup on the saucer. "I've never understood what he saw in that woman. I wish he'd had the sense to shoot her. That lie she told about him calling to say he was on his way to the house to kill her. What man would warn a stupid woman he was coming up to kill her? Although, Daisy could drive anyone to murder. Except *Wade*." She made it sound like a flaw in her brother's character.

Charity took a bite of her cookie. Lydia did make the most amazing sugar cookies. "What is the flavoring you put in these?" she asked, wondering if this was why Lydia had called her, to talk about Wade.

"It's my secret ingredient." Lydia took a sip of tea, then put down her cup, drawing herself up in the wheelchair. "I didn't call you over to talk about Wade or that woman he married. I need a favor."

Uh-oh.

Lydia leaned forward and whispered, ''Have you seen that man Betty is with?''

''Bruno?'' Everyone in town was talking about him. Drove an old trashed-out car and warmed a barstool at the Duck-In bar when he wasn't hanging out at Betty's bumming free meals.

''Bruno. Is that his name? Well, I've noticed him walking by the shop and looking in as if he were casing the joint,'' Lydia said.

Casing the joint?

''What do you know about him?'' she asked.

''Nothing.'' Charity was still trying to imagine Bruno ''casing'' the antique store. Sure, there were some valuable pieces and some small collectibles but she doubted Bruno would know the good stuff from the junk. And if he stole a pricey ornate oak buffet, how would he carry it? On his back? It certainly wouldn't fit in that old car of his.

''I want you to find out everything you can about him,'' Lydia said, glancing toward the front window.

Charity knew her shock must have shown. The Busy Bee was anything but busy this time of year and as far as Charity knew, Lydia never had more than a little cash in the till. Most people paid with credit cards or checks and that was when there was actually a customer. ''I really don't—'' Charity hedged.

''There he is,'' Lydia whispered.

Charity turned in time to see Bruno walk by. He was a large, not bad-looking man, with a thick head of shaggy blond hair. Bruno looked to be in his forties—a good ten years younger than Betty. Just the way she liked them.

"If you really think he's planning to rob you, shouldn't you talk to Jesse?" Charity suggested. "He's filling in as deputy until Mitch is well enough to go back to work."

Lydia was shaking her head. "I would look like a silly old woman crying wolf. No, I need to know more about him before I say anything to anyone but you. You're the one with the talent for finding out everything about everyone."

Compliments worked every time. "Okay, I could do some checking on him," Charity said.

"Good," Lydia said, sounding relieved. "He...scares me."

"Angus would never let anything happen to you."

"Angus is a dear but he is no spring chicken," Lydia said.

Angus still looked plenty capable of protecting his mistress. He had always been a large, muscular man and he'd stayed in shape, which made him seem younger than his sixtysomething years.

"I also have my own pistol in my nightstand," Lydia added with a glint in her eyes. "A woman can't be too careful. Especially one with my...disabilities."

There was a sound behind them on the back stairs, a door opening, footfalls as someone came down the steps toward them. It had to be Angus. He never used the elevator Wade had put in for Lydia.

"Don't say anything about Bruno to Angus," Lydia whispered. "Or about my gun. I hate to worry the old dear."

Angus appeared from behind a cloth curtain. "You

need anything from the store, Lydia?'' he inquired in that wonderful English accent Charity adored.

''No, thank you, Angus.''

''I'll only be a short while,'' he said and, nodding to Charity, left by the back door.

''He thinks I should sell the store, you know. Angus,'' she added as if Charity wasn't following. ''He says I should travel while I can still enjoy it and that he would gladly take me around the world if I like. Did you know he's quite wealthy in his own right. But how can I leave Wade especially now when he needs me?''

''He might be going to prison,'' Charity pointed out before she could catch herself.

''Yes,'' Lydia said. ''I guess then there would be nothing but the store keeping me here.''

''I should get going,'' Charity said, rising to her feet.

''Here, take a couple of cookies for later and maybe a few for Mitch?''

Charity could never turn down cookies. As she left, munching one of the cookies on her way to the newspaper office, she had an uneasy feeling about Lydia's fears over Bruno.

Chapter Seven

After leaving Desiree at Betty's, Jesse cruised around town, too restless to go back to the office. Timber Falls was dead. It had been weeks since there'd been a bigfoot sighting and it was still the rainy season so there were only locals left in town and most of those had holed up to wait out spring.

Jesse always thought it was the isolation and the cabin fever—locked inside for months while it rained day in and day out—that caused the craziness in Timber Falls. It was one of the reasons he'd gone to Mexico.

But it was his family that had brought him home. He could put up with the rain, he told himself. In a few months tourists would descend on the town to escape the heat in the valleys and residents would take a large collective sigh as if saying, ''Made it through another one.''

He made a wider circle around the small town. He didn't kid himself. He was looking for Maggie and her fancy motorcycle.

Common sense told him she wouldn't be hanging

around Timber Falls. Not with thousands of dollars in one of her saddlebags and an APB out on her. But what was she doing even passing through this time of year? If she was headed out of the country, she was taking the long route. Timber Falls wasn't even off secondary roads.

But a biker *could* disappear in the woods around here if she wanted to though. Or needed to.

What bothered him was the feeling that she hadn't left. That coming to Timber Falls hadn't been just a flip of the coin or a wrong turn.

IT DIDN'T TAKE Charity long to get the lowdown on Bruno once she had his real name and even that was pretty simple once she had the license plate number off his old car.

His name was Jerome Lovelace. That explained why he preferred Bruno.

For a moment she thought about asking Jesse to run a check on Lovelace, but she knew he would tell Mitch and she didn't want to worry Mitch. He hated it when she got involved in anything even remotely dangerous. Also she had her own sources.

She called her friend who worked at one of the Oregon law enforcement agencies and waited while Nancy tapped the computer keys and chewed nervously at her gum.

"Whoo-whee," Nancy whispered. "This boy's got a rap sheet as long as my arm."

"What kind of offenses? Any burglary or robbery?"

"Looks mostly like driving while intoxicated, drunk

and disorderly, aggravated assault, domestic abuse, driving without a valid license, driving without insurance. He did some time for criminal mischief and for fraud. Most are just misdemeanors. The guy's a loser."

"I gathered that just looking at him." Definitely Betty's type.

"Oh, here's one. He got picked up for fencing stolen goods but got off," Nancy said. "Doesn't say what kind of goods."

"How about last known address?"

"A post office box in Seattle. You want it?"

"No." Seattle? So what had brought him to Timber Falls? Fencing stolen goods. Like antiques, she wondered. "Thanks. I owe you."

"So true."

Charity hung up and considered what she'd learned. Maybe Bruno wanted to advance his criminal career. Maybe he was contemplating burglary. But Charity didn't buy it.

She grabbed her purse and, leaving the newspaper office, started down the street toward the Busy Bee antique shop. As she neared the shop, she slowed. Wasn't that Bruno ahead of her?

She ducked into one of the store entrances as he started to look over his shoulder. She didn't think he'd seen her. She waited a minute, then peered around the corner of the building and down Main Street.

Bruno had just reached the Busy Bee. She scooted up the street, keeping to the edge of the buildings.

He slowed, looking into the large plate-glass windows at the front of the antique shop, then swung into the entryway as if also not wanting to be seen.

Charity's heart was in her throat. Was it possible Lydia was right? That Bruno really did plan to rob the place?

Bruno had disappeared from view. She ran up the street after him. Had he gone into the antique shop or was he just hidden in the recessed entrance?

Was it possible he'd spotted her, thought she was following him and was waiting for her?

She was almost to the setback entry of the shop. She glanced toward the window, pretending to study her reflection critically in the glass.

Bruno was inside the shop. He was admiring a purple vase, one Charity remembered as being marked four hundred dollars—certainly more than Bruno could afford, she would bet.

But it wasn't Lydia waiting on him. It was Angus. He was frowning, obviously suspicious of the man and maybe a little wary that Bruno might drop the expensive vase and have no way to pay for it.

As Charity walked on past the shop, she saw Angus snatch the vase from him and put it back. Angus looked up and saw her. With a small nod, he watched her pass. Bruno turned, too, frowning. A moment later Charity heard the shop doorbell tinkle behind her, heard the heavy footsteps and knew it was Bruno.

She pushed into the Spit Curl, pulled the door closed after her. She hadn't realized she was holding her breath until she saw Bruno's shadow fall across the front window, then retreat on down the street.

"You look like you've seen a ghost," Mary Jane

Clark said from the beauty-shop chair. Mary Jane was getting a blond dye job to her dark roots.

As she watched Bruno saunter on up the street toward Betty's, Charity ignored Mary Jane just as she had throughout high school when Mary Jane had shown an interest in Mitch.

Bruno peered back just once and smiled as if he knew Charity was watching him. Clearly, he was enjoying her fear.

AFTER NOT FINDING a brightly colored motorcycle or the woman who'd been riding it, Jesse returned to his office, wondering if Detective Rupert Blackmore would be waiting for him. Or at least have called.

"She already made bail," Sissy said as Jesse walked into the office.

He didn't have to ask who she was. Daisy Dennison. He'd known she would be out before the fingerprint ink dried.

Sissy handed him another stack of messages. He flipped through them. None from Blackmore. He'd been so sure the cop would have all inquiries red-flagged. Maybe Blackmore really did just want to talk to Maggie about the murder. Maybe she wasn't a suspect.

But there were lots of messages from whiners about everything from a nasty smell coming from the neighbor's garbage cans to cars parked incorrectly along Main Street.

"Damn, don't these people have anything else to do?" he said as he headed for his office.

Sissy gave him her some-deputy-you-are look.

He sat down behind the desk and began making calls, pretending he was Mitch, pretending diplomacy was his middle name. Before he realized it, the afternoon had turned into evening. Sissy stuck her head in the door to say she was leaving and it was time to ante up for the next morning's doughnuts.

It wasn't until he'd gotten to the bottom of the pile of messages that he found Detective Rupert Blackmore's name and number where he'd scribbled it down earlier. He vaguely remembered doing it—just before he'd seen Desiree speed by.

If the cop was tagging inquiries, then he already knew that Maggie had been in Timber Falls. If the detective was really concerned, he would have called.

So a phone call from Jesse wouldn't make any difference at this point since she was long gone anyway.

But with one phone call, Jesse would know why the detective wanted to talk to Maggie. It would satisfy his curiosity. He started to pick up the phone. Hesitated. What was he afraid he was going to find out? It wasn't fear holding him back and he knew it. He knew he was crazy for not calling. Not to mention irresponsible. But his gut instincts were telling him to wait. And he'd always gone with his instincts. Right or wrong.

His stomach rumbled. He glanced at his watch. The detective wouldn't be in his office this late. Maybe in the morning. His stomach rumbled again. And Jesse had just enough time to get to Betty's before she closed. Idly, he wondered what Maggie Randolph was having for dinner tonight.

"WILL YOU BE all right alone for a little while?" Charity asked from the doorway.

"Call Florie again and you're dead," Mitch said from his recliner.

She smiled at him. "I was desperate."

"Uh-huh. You were paying me back for the times I insisted Florie stay with you." He motioned her closer, reached out and pulled her down to him. She was never more beautiful than when she was hot on a story. Unfortunately, he knew the look all too well. "Want to tell me about it?"

"Not yet." She smiled that secret little smile of hers, the one that gave him ulcers.

The only reason she wouldn't tell him would be if she thought he would try to stop her because it was dangerous. Damn. He wished he *could* stop her. But he'd been here before and knew stopping Charity was like trying to rein in a speeding bullet. He reminded himself that this was his future, worrying about Charity. "Be *careful.*"

She kissed him. "You know me."

He groaned but didn't let go of her, trailing kisses along her silken throat. At least this story had gotten her mind off the wedding. She'd been driving him crazy with discussions about orchids versus roses versus daisies let alone all the choices for the reception.

If that wasn't bad enough, Florie had to start warning Charity about bad luck wedding superstitions. Charity pretended she wasn't superstitious. Uh-huh. But then later she'd asked him if he'd seen a blind man, a monk or a pregnant woman on his way to the Dennison's the night he was shot.

All it seemed were bad luck before a proposal of marriage. But if he'd seen nanny goats, pigeons or wolves, then this would be a good omen that would bring good fortune to the marriage.

"I saw an entire flock of pigeons," he said, which made Charity laugh, but also look secretly relieved.

"Promise me that you'll call me at the paper if you need anything," she said now, her voice breaking a little as he nibbled at her ear.

"Promise."

She kissed him, a slow, sensuous kiss that made him desperately want to take her in his arms and make love to her. But even if he could with the cast and bandages, Charity was holding out for their wedding night.

He let go of her, not about to disappoint her now. She would get the wedding she wanted. A white one. And everyone knew "married in white, she'd chosen right."

The moment she was gone though, he called Jesse.

"I'd venture to guess she's chasing something to do with the Dennisons," Mitch told him. Charity had been chasing one story or another about them ever since she started the *Cascade Courier* right out of college. When news was slow there was always the town's only big mystery: the disappearance of Angela Dennison twenty-seven years before. It had become the stuff local legends are made of and Charity couldn't pass up a good mystery.

"Charity went to see Lydia Abernathy this afternoon," Mitch told his brother. Florie had slipped and told him. "And now she's headed for the newspaper office." With Lydia being Wade Dennison's sister he figured whatever reason she'd wanted to see Charity couldn't be good.

"Kinda late to be going to the newspaper. Damn, that woman is obstinate, isn't she," Jesse said, unable to hide the admiration in his voice. "Glad I'm not marrying her."

"Sure you are. Are you still in town?"

"I'm at Betty's." She was making him a sandwich to go. It had been the kind of day that made him anxious to get home and as far away from being a deputy as he could. Except he wouldn't sleep once he got home anyway. "You want me to check on Charity? No problem."

"Thanks. I'd suggest taking Charity a piece of pie. Banana cream, if Betty still has some. That way Charity won't take your head off."

Jesse grinned to himself as he hung up. It was great seeing his brother in love—and admitting it. If Mitch could fall so hard, wasn't there a chance for Jesse to find true love?

Betty bagged up the sandwich, a slice of banana cream and a slice of cherry for him.

As he drove down Main to the newspaper office, Charity was just getting out of her VW. He pulled in beside her and got out. "Here, let me get that for you," he said as she started to unlock the office. He smiled and, holding the bag from Betty's in one hand, took the keys from her.

"Mitch called you," she accused, not sounding pleased about it.

Jesse tried to look innocent, gave up and said, "I have pie. Banana cream."

She tried to hide a smile as he opened the door for her and turned on the light. "You can tell Mitch—" She stopped in midsentence, her eyes widening as she surveyed her office.

The newspaper was small, the office consisting of only three desks, a light table, copy machine, darkroom and a small press.

Everything looked fine to him. "What's wrong?"

Charity said nothing, just walked slowly into the room and headed straight for one of the large filing cabinets against the wall. The top drawer was open and when he looked past her, he saw a newspaper clipping lying on the floor between Charity and the darkroom.

He moved to her, touched her arm and motioned for her to be quiet as he headed toward the darkroom. Using his shirttail, he turned the knob. The door swung in. He flicked on the light.

The metal grate that covered a large air vent in the ceiling hung down exposing a gaping hole to the roof.

Dragging up a chair, Jesse peered into the ventilation system, careful not to touch anything. The opening was accessible from the roof and large enough for a small person to crawl through. He climbed down and checked the back door. It wasn't just unlocked. It wasn't even latched. He glanced down the alley. Empty.

"You always lock the back door?" he asked Charity.

She nodded. She hadn't moved, seemed to be frozen in her spot, eyes still wide. He figured she was reliving the last time someone had broken into the newspaper.

That time she'd been in the darkroom and the burglar had grabbed her, bound her with duct tape and stuffed her in the storage closet. Obviously that incident had made a lasting impression on her.

"The door was definitely locked," she said in a whisper.

"Well, it looks like your intruder came through the air vent on the roof down into the darkroom and then made a hasty retreat out the back door. Could have been a kid—"

"No," she interrupted, shaking her head and seeming to pull herself together. "A kid wouldn't break in to steal a file of newspaper clippings. One of my files is missing."

He frowned. "How can you tell that?"

She didn't answer, just moved to the clipping on the floor and using the pencil she'd picked up, she flipped the article over.

The headline read: Whatever Happened To Baby Angela?

Charity motioned toward the computer on the desk. Even from here he could see that the burglar had typed in the search keyword KIDNAPPING to access the file number.

"Someone is interested in the Angela Dennison case," she said.

"The file is missing?"

She nodded.

He swore under his breath. His bad feeling from earlier had settled deep in his gut.

"Interested enough to break in rather than wait until the office was open," Charity was saying. "Obviously, he doesn't want us to know who he is or why he's interested."

"Any idea who it could be?" he asked, hoping there was some weirdo in town who'd shown an interest in the case who was nuts enough to break in to read the file in private. No such luck.

She shook her head.

"Well, I think we scared whoever it was away, but there is no way you're staying here alone tonight to work."

Charity surprised him by not arguing. "It can wait until tomorrow."

Clearly she saw the potential for another story after this break-in. "You want to dust this clipping?" she asked.

He nodded and saw her glance at the sack from Betty's. "Just take the banana cream. The cherry pie and sandwich is mine."

She grinned at him as she drew out the carton with the slice of cream pie inside and took a whiff, closing her eyes for a moment, a smile on her lips.

"My brother is one lucky man."

She opened her eyes. "You know it."

Jesse walked her out to her car. "Straight home?"

"You're going to call Mitch the moment I pull away, aren't you?"

He smiled. "You know it." He watched her drive away, then took the investigation kit out of the back of the patrol car. He'd seen Mitch do this a few times and figured at this point there was no reason to call in the state crime lab boys. Not yet anyway.

He got a half dozen latents off the newspaper clipping and one good clear one from the back doorknob. He was hoping the burglar had taken off his gloves to peek at the articles. Maybe he hadn't planned to steal the file, didn't want to throw up a red flag when Charity found it missing.

So when he heard Jesse's and Charity's cars pull up out front after everything in town was closed and the sidewalks practically rolled up for the night, he'd just grabbed the file and run, dropping the one clipping and leaving a print on the back doorknob.

Of course there was a good chance the prints would all turn out to be Charity's. Or Blaine's, the high-school kid who worked for her.

BACK AT HIS OFFICE, Jesse called Mitch. Charity had made it home safe and sound although Mitch was upset that someone had broken into the newspaper office, especially after the last time.

"Can you walk me through the process for sending fingerprints to the state lab?" Jesse asked his brother, taking a bite of his sandwich and booting up the computer.

Jesse did as he was instructed, figuring it would take a while to get an ID, if he got one at all tonight.

But to his surprise, the results came up immediately. He let out a curse and pushed the remaining sandwich aside.

"What?" Mitch said on the other end of the line.

"I didn't think they would come back so fast," Jesse told him. One print, the one from the back door, had come up with a match.

"That means there's an APB out on this person," Mitch said.

No kidding. The clean print on the back doorknob belonged to Margaret Jane Randolph of West Seattle.

"Tell me Charity hasn't gotten herself into trouble," Mitch said.

"Not to worry, little brother," Jesse said. No reason to tell him about Maggie just yet. "I'll call and see what's up and get back to you in the morning." He hung up before Mitch could argue.

Jesse stared at the number on the screen. Damn. Maggie wasn't on her way to Mexico. She was busy breaking into the newspaper to read the Angela Dennison file. For some reason this woman on the run from a murder investigation had stopped long enough to read a newspaper file on kidnapping.

Now what kind of sense did that make? None. And yet, it made perfect sense to him.

He opened the container with the cherry pie inside and took a few bites before he dialed the telephone number he'd scribbled down earlier. It was way too late but maybe big city detectives worked late.

Maggie had broken into his soon-to-be sister-in-law's newspaper. It was high time he found out just what the hell was the story with his mystery biker.

He got Detective Rupert Blackmore's voice mail. Blackmore had a deep, rough-sounding voice. An older cop, hardened from time and the streets, Jesse thought. He'd met a few of them. He hung up without leaving a message.

"Now why the hell did you do that?" he asked himself and swore.

He couldn't explain it. Just a gut feeling that he needed to talk to Maggie Randolph before he talked to the cop.

Disgusted with himself, he got up from the desk and went to the window. "Some deputy you are." He stared out at the dark night. It had started to rain again. Soon he would have webbed feet if he stayed in this town.

He'd have to find her. Find out what the hell she was doing in Timber Falls. What she was searching for. But he had a bad feeling he already knew, had known longer than he wanted to admit.

Chapter Eight

In the dark tent, Maggie stared at the thick file. Her heart was still pounding. That had been a close call back at the newspaper. She'd never expected anyone to show up, not after hours and certainly not in a town that was dead by eight at night.

How long would it take the deputy to find out that she'd broken into the paper and taken the Angela Dennison file? How long before he notified Blackmore?

She should have left the file, but there wasn't time to cover her tracks, and she had to know what was in it. She'd only just started reading through the clippings, hiding in the darkroom with her flashlight, when she'd heard the cars pull up out front.

Would they have realized by now that she took the file? Maybe not. Maybe no one would know for a while. But if it came out, then Blackmore would not only know she was in town but that she'd stumbled onto the truth.

She shone the flashlight on the file, her fingers brushing the bulging worn folder. It seemed she had been the news for twenty-seven years.

After reading for a few minutes, there was no doubt in her mind that she was the baby who had been kidnapped twenty-seven years ago from her crib in a house a few miles from here. She was Angela Dennison, youngest daughter of Wade and Daisy Dennison, owners of Dennison Ducks, a plant where decoys were carved.

The file contained not only articles published by the *Cascade Courier*, but copies of ones from larger newspapers where the kidnapping had made front page news when it happened years ago.

Angela Dennison was only a few weeks old when she was taken from her crib in the dark of night, never to be seen again. Not only was Angela the same age as Maggie, they shared the same birthday—March ninth.

And Maggie had been adopted not twenty-four hours after Angela Dennison's disappearance.

Many of the local stories had been written by Charity Jenkins for the *Cascade Courier*. She read through all the articles again. If she was right she was the daughter of the most written about family in town.

Maggie put the articles back in the file and snapped off the light, plunging the tent in darkness. Her head ached and she felt sick to her stomach. Closing her eyes, she listened to the sound of the river and the wind in the trees…and the frantic beat of her heart.

It was all mind-blowing. According to the articles, the mystery had been solved a few months ago when the plant production manager had been killed after admitting to Charity Jenkins right before he died that he had taken the baby. But it was clear from the newspaper articles written after his death that he had not acted alone.

Apparently both parents, Daisy and Wade Dennison, had been suspects. Might still be suspects. She had studied the photo of Wade and Daisy Dennison for a long time. It was a black-and-white, grainy and not clear enough to see any resemblance.

Or maybe she just didn't want to see a resemblance. Didn't want to be part of this infamous family.

As she sat in the darkness, she tried to tell herself it could be worse. Wade Dennison was in jail for shooting the Timber Falls sheriff during a recent domestic dispute with his estranged wife Daisy. How could it be worse than that?

Maggie felt hot tears on her cheeks. She hadn't let herself cry. Not at the pier when Norman had been killed. Not after, when she knew it was only a matter of time before Blackmore caught up with her.

She'd focused on only one thing: learning the truth. Once she knew, she'd thought that she would be safe.

But now she saw that that wasn't the case. She still had no idea why Blackmore wanted her dead. Her throat constricted as she fought back the sobs that made her chest ache. Scared and tired and sick over what she'd found, she curled around the pain as the sobs racked her body and tears burned down her cheeks.

She was Angela Dennison. Like it or not. And for some reason, her life was in danger because of it.

After a few minutes, she dried her tears and pulled herself together. Enough crying. She couldn't just hide out in this tent and feel sorry for herself.

If Blackmore had been behind the kidnapping, that would explain why he didn't want the truth coming out. So he must have had some connection to Timber Falls. All she had to do was find it.

The obvious place to start seemed to be her biological family. Wade Dennison was a powerful man in this town but he was in jail. Was it possible he had influence as far away as Seattle? Or was it his wife Daisy who might have known Blackmore?

Maggie turned on the flashlight long enough to hide the stolen file under her mat, then pocketing the light, she left the tent and headed for her bike. She had hours before daylight and a lot to do before then. It was only a matter of time before Blackmore found out she was in Timber Falls and came to finish what he'd started.

DETECTIVE RUPERT BLACKMORE was tired and cranky and his whole body ached after driving for hours. He still had miles to go to get to Timber Falls, Oregon. A waitress in an all-night truck stop refilled his coffee cup. He'd drunk too much coffee to try to stay awake and his stomach was killing him.

"Can I get you anything else?" she asked, drawing her order pad from her uniform pocket. She didn't look up as she tore off his bill and laid it on the table. She glanced at him then.

"No." He shook his head. "Thank you."

She gave him a smile, a granddaughterly smile. "Good luck. Hope you catch a bunch."

He watched her walk away. Hope you catch a bunch. Fish. She'd gotten the idea that he was going fishing no doubt from his hat with the lures on it and the old jacket and flannel shirt he was wearing. He smiled to himself.

Yesterday, he'd only gone home long enough to take a shower, change his clothing and collect several of the unregistered weapons he'd picked up over the years. At least the weapons weren't registered to him. They'd been ones he'd found at drug busts, ones tossed out of moving vehicles he'd chased down, ones he'd taken off dead gang members. Ones that could never be traced back to him.

At first he'd just collected them, like trophies of wild game kills. At least he thought he had. But maybe he'd known all along that the day would come when he would need a gun.

Blackmail was an insidious thing. Even when you didn't hear from the blackmailer for years, you always knew the day would come when payment would be demanded. And unless you wanted your entire world to unravel like the yarn of a slashed sweater, then you paid—no matter the price.

He'd taken the pickup he used for his fishing trips. Thrown in his tent for good measure, along with his fishing jacket and hat. When he'd finally gotten everything loaded into the pickup and slipped behind the wheel, the fishing hat perched on his head, he'd glanced in the rearview mirror.

He'd been shocked at how much he'd aged. It was as if his hair and beard had turned completely gray overnight. When was the last time he'd looked into the mirror, really looked? Obviously not when he shaved in the morning.

He recalled old fishermen he'd met over the years,

tottering along the edge of the water, squinting into the sun from a face wrinkled and weathered with age and water and wind, and realized he could have been one of them.

That's when it hit him. What the people of Timber Falls, Oregon, would see. An old fisherman. Not a cop.

Not unless they looked into his eyes. That was the only part of him that would give him away. The life-hardened ice-blue eyes that even he didn't like to look into.

He'd picked up a pair of sunglasses off the dash of the truck, put them on and looked in the mirror again. He couldn't have picked a better disguise.

He left the waitress a good tip, paid his bill at the cash register and bought himself two of the best cigars the truck stop had to offer. As he headed for his pickup, he felt better than he had in days.

Maggie Randolph would never see him coming.

JESSE STARED at the computer in the empty office. He knew he should go home and try to get some sleep. He could start looking for Maggie in the morning.

He leaned toward the computer, remembering what Sissy had shown him. Maggie Randolph had broken into the newspaper to research the Angela Dennison kidnapping case. While Charity's paper was too small to have an online morgue, a large paper in the Seattle area would, wouldn't it?

He went online, called up one of the two largest newspapers there, typed in the name Margaret Randolph and waited. Maybe there wouldn't be anything on her. Maybe she hadn't lived there long enough. Maybe—

A long list of articles appeared on the screen. He scanned down them surprised that most had run on the sports pages. He shook his head in wonder. It seemed Maggie liked to race motorcycles, participate in extreme skiing competitions and scuba dive in dangerous waters. How about that?

He started back up the list, spotted one marked Obit and clicked on it. Maggie's name was listed as the only surviving child of Paul Randolph who had been killed in a plane crash less than two months ago. He started to click off the obituary when he spotted another one farther down. He clicked on it. Again Maggie's name was listed as the only child. The obit was for Mildred Randolph, Maggie's mother. He skimmed it, noted that the mother had contracted polio as a child and had been in a wheelchair, and at the bottom saw something that made him catch his breath.

Memorials were to be made to an organization the Randolphs had started to assist older, disabled couples in adopting a child.

What were the odds that Maggie was adopted?

Jesse swore, more sure than ever he was on the right track. He moved the cursor back to the top of the list and clicked on the most recent article under Margaret Jane Randolph.

It was a story about a legal assistant named Norman Drake. His body had been fished out of the water near an abandoned pier on Puget Sound this morning. His death was being investigated as a homicide. Margaret Randolph was wanted for questioning in the man's murder along with that of Drake's boss, a local attorney named Clark Iverson who was murdered in his office last week. Iverson had been a longtime family friend and attorney for Randolph's father, the recently deceased Paul Randolph.

Jesse let out a low whistle. Maggie seemed to have left a trail of bodies behind her. And now she was in Timber Falls doing a little B and E to research an old kidnapping case?

Locking up the office, Jesse climbed on his bike. It was late but there was something that couldn't wait. He'd put it off for too many years already.

LEE TANNER came out onto his deck, squinting into the darkness, as Jesse shut off his motorcycle. "Son, I was hoping that was you."

Jesse saw with relief that his father was sober. It had been a long time now but he wondered if he would always feel that instant of fear just before the relief no matter how many years his father had been on the wagon. "I know it's late...."

Lee shook his head. "I'm glad you stopped by. I was just enjoying the night sky." The rain shower had passed, leaving the sky clear and full of stars.

Jesse joined him at the deck railing, trying to see his father the way Daisy Dennison must have almost thirty years ago. Lee still had a thick head of dark hair, but at fifty-five it was shot with silver. When Lee Tanner used to ride horses in the woods behind the house with Daisy his hair had been as black as Jesse's.

His father was still an attractive man, strong and lean, his dark eyes more solemn than Jesse remembered them, his demeanor more serene. Was that just from being sober? Or had his father found some kind of peace with the past?

Jesse was reminded that he'd thought the same thing of Daisy, that the years had mellowed her, as well.

"What's on your mind, son?" Lee asked, tilting his head back as he looked up at the glittering stars and sliver of silver moon overhead. A light breeze stirred the tops of the nearby pines, whispering softly to the night.

Jesse hesitated, afraid he was about to destroy any peace his father had found and send him back to the bottle. "The newspaper office was broken into tonight."

Lee looked over at him in surprise. This rainy season had been the worst. Murders and shootings and all interrelated in some way to the Dennisons.

"The burglar took Angela Dennison's kidnapping file." Jesse saw his father tense. A deep silence stretched between them. "There's something I need to ask you."

"As a lawman or my son?" Lee inquired quietly.

"Both. I need to know if there is any chance Angela Dennison is your daughter."

Lee closed his eyes and sighed softly. "Why would you ask me that after all these years? What possible difference could it make now?"

"I think she's alive," Jesse said, the words tumbling out, words he hadn't dared even think let alone say until this moment. "I think she's in Timber Falls. And I think she's in bad trouble. I have to know the truth. It might be the only way I can help her."

His father's eyes came open slowly. He stared at his son, his whole body seeming to quake as he gripped the rail. "Angela alive?" Tears welled in his dark eyes, now no longer at peace. "Does Daisy know?"

"I don't even know for sure myself yet," Jesse said, but maybe part of him had known from the moment Maggie had lifted her head beside that rain-soaked highway last night and he'd felt as if he'd been hit between the eyes with a two-by-four. He hadn't wanted to see the resemblance. So like Desiree and yet so different.

"My God, if Angela really is alive..." Lee Tanner stumbled over to one of the deck chairs and lowered himself into it, looking suddenly older than his fifty-five years.

"I have to know, Dad."

His father was shaking his head in wonder, staring off into the darkness as if caught in the past again. "Everyone thought she was dead."

"Dad? Is there a chance that Angela is your daughter?"

Lee Tanner looked up. "It's been so long, Jesse. You have to understand, we're different people than we were then. I know part of you believes the affair was why your mother left me—"

"I don't care about that. I *have* to know if Angela could be your daughter. My...half sister."

"Why would the truth ever have to come out? What difference—" Lee Tanner seemed to see the answer in Jesse's gaze. "Don't tell me that you're—"

"I've only laid eyes on her once," Jesse said quickly. "But if I'm right about her..." How could he explain to his father that he was instantly drawn to this woman, felt things he'd never felt? He couldn't explain it to himself. And his greatest fear was that this woman would always be forbidden to him.

"Oh, Jesse."

"I need to know the time frame."

His father seemed about to deny it, then said quietly, "I honestly don't know. But it's possible both girls could be mine."

Desiree, too. Hadn't Jesse always suspected as much? Wasn't that why he'd never taken her up on her many offers? Why he'd felt brotherly toward her?

Well, he didn't feel that way toward Maggie.

"Didn't you ever bother to ask Daisy?" he demanded.

His father looked up at him. "She went back to Wade for a while and swore that Desiree was his."

"And Angela?"

"We never spoke about Angela."

Jesse cursed under his breath. "When did Daisy break it off?"

His father seemed surprised by the question. "Daisy didn't. I did."

So that's how it had gone down. Mitch told him not long ago that Daisy had said she loved their father. Did she still? "When was that?"

"Before I knew she was pregnant," he said and looked out across the dense forest that stretched in front of his place. "I couldn't keep having an affair, not while I was married to your mother. I knew it was wrong but Daisy and I— I suppose that's why Daisy never told me she was pregnant. I didn't talk to her again until—''

''Until my mother left,'' Jesse guessed. ''Daisy must have called you to tell you that your wife had been up to the house demanding blackmail money.''

Lee closed his eyes again in silent acknowledgement.

''That's when you changed your mind and gave her the money to leave,'' Jesse said, seeing now how it had happened. His mother had never loved his father. As far back as he could remember, Jesse knew she wanted to leave the three of them, had just waited for her husband to grant her a divorce—and pay her off.

His father said nothing. What could he say about a woman who was that desperate to abandon her two sons and husband and had been long before her husband had taken up with Daisy Dennison.

''Why did Daisy tell you about mother going up there?'' Wasn't it obvious? ''She wanted you to face how badly my mother wanted to leave, didn't she?''

He opened his eyes. ''Ruth was a good woman—''

''Don't even try to sell me on her, okay?''

Lee looked down at his boots. All these years he'd tried to spare Jesse and Mitch, pretending their mother had wanted them, just couldn't handle marriage to him, always blaming himself and making excuses for her.

''Did Daisy hope you two would resume your affair after that?'' Jesse asked.

A few minutes stretched past. ''Daisy wanted more than I could offer her then.''

That surprised Jesse. Was it possible his dad had been serious about Daisy?

"Whatever Daisy was thinking, Angela's kidnapping changed everything for her," Lee Tanner continued, turning to look at Jesse. "If this woman really is Angela..."

Jesse nodded. "It could open up a can of worms that will make everything else pale by comparison."

They fell into a deep silence again.

Jesse reached into his jacket pocket and handed his father the DNA test. "I need this now."

He nodded, went into the house and returned a few minutes later. He handed his son the boxed up test. It was hard to tell what his father was thinking, let alone feeling at that moment.

"If I'm right, a lot more than dirty laundry is going to come out," Jesse said. "There's been some deaths back in the city where she's been living."

His father's eyes widened. "You don't think she—"

"No. She isn't a killer." How did he know that? He just did. Just like he knew she was Angela Dennison. "I'm afraid she's in trouble." Hell, he *knew* she was in trouble—that saddlebag full of money, the APB out on her. He just didn't know how much.

He looked over at his father, saving the worst for last. "Dad, I need to know where my mother is."

Lee reared back as if he'd been punched. "Why would you—"

"Do you know where she is?" Jesse watched his father's face. "You do." Jesse groaned. "You've been sending her money all these years.'' He couldn't believe it.

''You're wrong. But I would have if she'd asked. She's your mother.''

''She was *never* a mother to Mitch and me and you know it.''

''She brought you into this world,'' Lee said. ''For that, I owe her. And so do you.''

Jesse gritted his teeth. ''Where is she?''

''You're asking as a deputy now, aren't you?''

''Yes. She could be a material witness in the kidnapping. She was at the Dennison house just before Angela disappeared and she was never questioned because she skipped town that same day.'' Jesse narrowed his eyes at his father. ''Don't tell me you haven't wondered if she had something to do with Daisy Dennison's baby disappearing.''

He expected his father to argue that Ruth Anne Tanner would never steal the woman's baby to get back at her because of the affair. He didn't. Couldn't. Even if Ruth hadn't given a damn about her husband, she had tried to blackmail Daisy. When Daisy threw her out without a cent, Ruth might have decided to get even and they both knew it.

''I don't know where she is,'' Lee said, his voice sounding hoarse. ''My only connection to her is through my attorney and hers.''

''Your attorney still Matthew Brooks?''

His father nodded with obvious reluctance. ''Jesse, please don't go see her. No good can come of it.''

''I don't doubt that,'' Jesse said, hearing the fear in his father's voice. Like Jesse, he must fear his former wife had kidnapped Angela and involved Bud Farnsworth out of vengeance?

Or maybe for money. It seemed Maggie had ended up with wealthy adoptive parents. He could only guess how that had happened. "This has been a long time coming. I'm sure you know that."

Lee wagged his head. "I don't want to see you boys hurt."

"Then don't tell Mitch," Jesse said. "I'll protect my little brother for as long as I can. But if my mother took that baby..."

Lee looked away. "For Daisy's sake I pray Angela really is alive and that your mother had nothing to do with taking her."

Jesse studied his father, seeing something that he'd missed years ago. Lee's feelings for Daisy Dennison. How deep did they run? Jesse wasn't sure he wanted to know.

"You won't say anything to Mitch about this?" he asked his father.

Lee looked up in surprise. "And have Charity find out? It would be on the front page of her paper by tomorrow." He smiled as if admiring her tenacity, the same tenacity that had her now about to marry Mitch. "No matter what you find out, son, we're a family. We'll weather this storm just like we have all the others."

Jesse nodded, wishing he could believe that. "Tell your lawyer I'll be contacting him."

Lee sighed and looked out into the darkness. "I hope you know what you're doing."

As Jesse walked back to his bike, a few white

clouds cruised by over the tops of the trees obscuring the stars and moon, darkening the night to as black as his mood. Maggie was out there somewhere. He could feel it. Fate had made their paths cross. But maybe not for the reason he'd originally thought. Or desperately wanted.

Either way, she needed him. And he doubted she realized it. He just hoped he could find her before it was too late.

As he reached to start the bike, he felt the damned cell phone vibrate in his pocket.

"Jesse!" Daisy Dennison cried the moment he answered the phone. "Someone has broken into Dennison Ducks. The thief is still there. The new production manager is on the other line calling from her cell phone outside the plant watching it happening right now. Someone's in Wade's office with a flashlight going through the files!"

"I'm on my way." Jesse snapped off the phone and headed the bike toward Dennison Ducks already pretty sure he knew who the thief was and what she was looking for.

Chapter Nine

Maggie had just dropped through the air vent into the second-story office section of Dennison Ducks, when she heard it. The soft scuff of a shoe on the concrete first floor below her.

She froze, listening. Had she only imagined it? She waited, heard nothing, then snapped on the small flash-light and shone it around the office.

Quickly and quietly she moved past the secretary's desk to Wade Dennison's office. Her light caught on an eye gleaming from the corner. Her heart leaped to her throat, choking off her scream. She settled the flashlight beam on the eye, ready to run.

A large duck, its plastic eye sparkling, looked back at her. She realized the room was full of ducks. Every size, shape and color stared down at her from a shelf that ran the entire circumference of the room.

Hurriedly, she scanned the file cabinets, not sure exactly what she was looking for until she spotted the locked file drawer directly behind his desk. She moved soundlessly to the desk, picked up the letter opener and approached the file drawer.

The lock was old, the cabinet handle dusty as if it hadn't been opened for a while. She pried with the letter opener until the lock broke and, holding the same flashlight in her teeth, quietly slid open the drawer.

That's when she heard the sound again. Someone moving through the plant below her. A stair creaked. Then another. Someone was coming up the steps to the office.

Deputy Jesse Tanner? Had someone spotted the light in the office and called the cops?

There was only one file in the drawer. The rest of the space was covered in dust. She grabbed the file, stuffed it into her jacket, turned off the flashlight and not bothering to close the drawer, retraced her steps quietly across the room.

She could hear someone coming up the steps now, see the faint glow of a penlight. She reached out in the dark, located the desk and climbed up onto it. Any moment the person would enter the office.

She froze, immobilized with fear, as she caught a whiff of the same odor she'd smelled on the pier right before Blackmore had tried to kill her.

He was almost to the top of the stairs. Maggie pulled herself up into the vent and moved fast, no longer afraid of making noise. She could hear the thunder of running footsteps across the office, the rattle of the vent grate as it was banged aside.

In an instant she was on the roof and racing across to the pine tree she'd climbed for access. She scrambled down through the limbs afraid someone would be waiting for her at the bottom.

But once on the ground, no one appeared out of the darkness.

She leaped onto her bike, started it quickly, taking off down the road at full speed. She hadn't gone far when she saw the headlight of the other bike. It came roaring up the hill, the headlight catching her broadside in its sights.

JESSE WAS almost to the decoy plant when he spotted the single light coming out. A biker. Moving fast.

In his headlight he saw the gleam of the biker's helmet, recognized both it and the bike as she turned to look in his direction. First the newspaper and now Dennison Ducks.

She saw him, turned hard to the right, throwing up gravel as she took a short cut across the ditch and flew up onto the dirt road headed away from town.

He went after her, telling himself she couldn't outrun him on this narrow rutted dirt road that wound through the mountains. She didn't know the road as well as he did. Nor could she take the familiar curves the way he could—and had on many occasions in his youth.

But then he'd forgotten that he wasn't dealing with just any woman. Maggie had been racing bikes since she was a girl. She stayed ahead of him no matter how hard he tried to catch her, hugging the corners, riding high on the road and staying in the lead.

Damn. He feared she would kill herself trying to get away from him and yet he had to catch her. He couldn't let her get away from him. Not again.

They roared through the darkness, the dense forest

rushing by, the road a winding ribbon of rutted dirt track.

He realized that the dirt road would soon connect to the main highway. The way she was riding and given the capabilities of her bike she'd outrun him once she hit pavement again.

He stayed right with her but just as he'd known once she roared up onto the highway she was gone, leaving his Harley in the dust.

He stopped, tore off his helmet and swore as the last red glow of her taillight faded in the distance. That woman could ride, but he'd known that about her.

He wondered, as he stared after her down the highway into the darkness, what else he would learn about Maggie Randolph before this was over—and that's what had him worried.

He shifted the cycle into gear and headed back toward Dennison Ducks. He still had to deal with Daisy before the night was over. But somewhere out there in the forest was a biker with a personal interest in Angela Dennison's kidnapping. A biker with a bunch of money in a saddlebag and a West Seattle homicide detective after her.

And he had no way to help her. Even a woman as capable as Maggie Randolph might be in more trouble than she could handle. He wondered when he'd see her again.

Not soon enough to suit him.

MAGGIE TOOK a series of back roads she'd memorized from the old logging road maps, putting as much distance as she could between her and the deputy. And the man who'd been in the decoy plant with her tonight.

Detective Blackmore wasn't just in Timber Falls. He'd been at Dennison Ducks. He'd been that close. Had he followed her to the decoy plant? Or had he just known that's where she would show up?

Her heart was still pounding. She'd smelled him. That same rank smell she'd caught on the pier just before he fired at her and she'd rolled off the pier with Norman's dead body and splashed down into the churning surf.

And right behind the killer had been Deputy Jesse Tanner. She'd known the moment she saw the single headlight who it was. She'd seen his bike in the garage, an old Harley. Had Detective Blackmore called him? Or had someone else?

She hadn't been sure she could outrun Jesse. It had been close until she reached the highway and opened her bike up.

Now she pulled over to the side of the logging road, shaken and weak from the fear. She shut off the engine to listen. The silence engulfed her like the darkness. She breathed in the night air and let it out slowly. She was safe. For the moment.

But now both Blackmore and the deputy knew she'd been at Dennison Ducks. Maybe even knew it had been her at the newspaper. Jesse Tanner was smart enough to put it together given her mode of entry into the buildings.

Detective Blackmore must have called the deputy to help him capture her under the pretense of taking her back to Seattle. And wouldn't Deputy Jesse Tanner have to give her over to Blackmore? Wasn't that the way the law worked?

Her heart rate began to slow. And she felt a stab of regret that Jesse hadn't caught her. That she hadn't *let* him catch her. By now she would know one way or the other if Blackmore had gotten to the deputy.

That kind of thinking could get her killed, she reminded herself.

So why did her instincts tell her Deputy Jesse Tanner could be trusted? And with more than her life. Or maybe she just wanted to believe that because she liked him. She smiled at that understatement.

JESSE FOUND Daisy's new production manager waiting outside the back door at Dennison Ducks.

He parked his bike and walked toward the woman, surprised in more ways than one. He'd heard Daisy was taking over the running of the decoy factory now that Wade was in jail, but as far as he knew there'd been no announcement of a new production manager since Bud Farnsworth had been killed there in October.

Since Daisy had never shown any interest in Dennison Ducks—other than spending the income from it—Jesse, like the rest of the town, wasn't sure what to expect from her as far as management skills.

"You must be Deputy Tanner," the woman said extending a hand. "Mrs. Dennison told me to wait for you here. I'm Frances Sanders, the new production manager."

Frances was tall and blond in her late fifties with a kind face and a strong grip.

Jesse shook her hand, trying hard to hide his surprise since he knew damned well that Wade would never have hired a woman for the position.

"You expected a man," Frances said with a smile. "Don't let my gender fool you. I know what I'm doing. My father was a decoy carver. I grew up in the business."

"Didn't mean to infer otherwise," he said and returned her smile. "You're just a lot different from the last production manager."

"I should hope so from what I've heard about him," she said smoothly, then looked toward the plant. "I came by to pick up some reports and saw a flashlight beam bobbing around inside the main plant and called Mrs. Dennison at once. A few minutes later, I saw the second flashlight."

"Second flashlight?" he asked in surprise.

She nodded. "There was definitely two of them. One on the lower floor, the second upstairs in Mrs. Dennison's office."

Mrs. Dennison's office? Formerly Wade's office.

"I got a glimpse of both of them as they were fleeing. The one who took off over the roof was small and slim, a woman I think. The other was definitely a man, larger."

Could he be wrong about Maggie? "They were *together?*"

She shook her head. "I got the impression the man was chasing the woman. She took off on a motorcycle, but you know that since I heard you go after her."

He smiled, impressed. "And the man?"

"Just caught a glimpse of him going through the

trees.'' She pointed in the opposite direction. ''Then I heard the sound of an engine. Truck, I'd say. Can't be sure, it was too far away.''

He nodded. ''Nice job. Have you been inside yet?''

''I waited for you. I didn't want to destroy any evidence.''

''Let's take a look.'' And he stood back while she opened the door.

It didn't take him long to find where someone had broken in through a window at the back. Maggie had come in through an air vent via the roof same as she had at the newspaper office. He'd known she hadn't come to steal decoys so finding what she'd been after was a no-brainer.

''Looks like the lock on the top drawer of the file cabinet has been broken,'' Frances noted.

The drawer was open as if Maggie had been interrupted again. The drawer was also empty but he could see where possibly one file folder had been. The rest of the drawer was covered in fine dust. It seemed odd that Wade would keep this drawer locked and yet it had held so little. ''Any idea what was kept in here?''

She shook her head. ''Only Mrs. Dennison could tell you that.''

Mrs. Dennison. He glanced around. Nothing else seemed to have been disturbed. What had Maggie been looking for? He could only guess. More information on Angela Dennison.

And what had the second intruder been after?

Maggie Randolph.

''Thanks for your help,'' he told Frances as she locked up after him. She was like a breath of fresh air compared to the last production manager. "Good luck with your new job."

Jesse had hoped he wouldn't have to see Daisy Dennison again. Twice in one day was way too much. But he climbed on his bike, deciding to get it over with tonight.

The Dennison mansion was a couple of miles from the decoy factory. As he turned onto the road that led to the house, he saw that all the lights were on, including the porch lamp. Daisy had obviously been expecting him. She answered the door herself after only one ring.

"Did you catch the thief?" She had a drink in her hand and she looked as if it wasn't her first.

"You mind if I come in?"

She looked contrite, stepped back and waved him inside. "What can I have Zinnia bring you to drink?"

"Nothing for me."

She seemed disappointed and he wondered if she got lonely in this big house with Desiree usually off getting into trouble. He wondered how Daisy would take the news if he was right about Maggie.

"As far as I can tell the only thing taken might have been a file from a locked cabinet in Wade's office," he told her.

Daisy looked down at her glass, then held it to her lips and took a drink.

"What was in that file?" he asked, seeing that she knew something about that locked filing cabinet drawer.

Turning her back on him she walked into the living

room. "Wade's...*personal* papers," she said over her shoulder.

Anger drove him deeper into the house. The place smelled of scotch and some too-sweet scented candle. He felt nauseous. "Let's not play games, okay? The newspaper was also broken into tonight. The burglar took only one thing. A file containing stories about Angela's kidnapping."

Daisy froze.

He could almost feel the tension emanating from her. "So I'll ask you again, what was in that file?"

When she spoke all the steel had gone out of her. "Why can't people just leave my family alone?"

He could think of several answers to that question starting with the family's bad behavior but he had a feeling the question was rhetorical. And he'd already shared his feelings with her earlier today. He doubted she'd put up with another lecture.

"Please," she said turning to look at him. "Sit down." As if on cue, the German housekeeper appeared with a tall glass of lemonade he hadn't asked for and another drink for her mistress.

Jesse took the chair Daisy offered him and the lemonade. It was better than his. "Great lemonade," he said to Zinnia's retreating back. She gave no sign that she'd heard him.

"She doesn't speak much English," Daisy said.

He nodded, figuring Zinnia spoke more than probably Daisy realized. He wondered what it took to live in the same house with these people let alone serve them the way Zinnia did. He shuddered to think.

"I'm not sure what was in the file," she said after

a moment. "I know that he kept the correspondence with private investigators during the many years we searched for Angela. False leads, dead ends. I guess Wade didn't want me to see it. He had the only key and the cabinet was always locked."

"Whatever secrets were in there, they're going to come out," he warned. "If there is anything you want to tell me..."

Daisy put down her unfinished drink and didn't pick up the new one. Her eyes were shiny with booze and possibly regret as she looked up at him as if she'd been somewhere else. "The DNA tests were in there," she said her voice barely a whisper.

"What DNA tests?"

"The one Wade took to prove that he was that woman's father. Hers was in there, too." Her voice was barely a whisper. The woman in question was the product of an affair Wade Dennison had had almost thirty years ago with the nanny.

So now Maggie had the DNA test results.

Daisy met his gaze. "You look more like your father than even Mitch does." She was crying as she started to reach for the intercom to buzz the housekeeper. "Zinnia will show you out."

"I can find my own way."

ONCE ON THE ROAD into town, Jesse opened up the bike and let it run. The night air was cold and damp. He watched the ribbon of dark road disappear under his front tire and felt that old pull.

But it wasn't as strong as it had once been. Instead,

his mind quickly shifted to Maggie Randolph as he reached the edge of town—and how to find her.

The Duck-In Bar was closing as he cruised through town on his way home. He was tired and was hoping for a few hours of sleep before he went looking for Maggie.

But as he passed the bar, he saw Desiree opening the passenger side of her red sports car. The top was up but he'd gotten a glimpse of the man behind the wheel.

He swore and flipped a U-turn in the middle of the street and went back.

Desiree turned at the sound of the bike; then smiled when she saw who it was and waited, holding the door open, not getting in just yet. Her gaze met his as if in defiance and she glanced toward the guy behind the wheel, no doubt wanting to make sure Jesse had seen who her date was. Bruno, the guy who'd been hanging out with Betty.

Jesse pulled alongside the car where Desiree was standing with the passenger door open. She seemed pleased that she'd gotten a reaction out of him. His contempt for her antics must have shown. Did his guilt show, as well? He couldn't help but think she was as confused as he was about their relationship and that of their parents.

"I was just at your house," he said. "Someone broke into Dennison Ducks. Your mother isn't doing too well."

The smile flickered and died. "Is Mom—"

"She's fine. Upset, obviously. Scared."

Desiree had paled. He could see that even under the

glow of the Duck-In neon. She closed the passenger door and started around the car to the driver's side. She opened the door and motioned without a word for Bruno to get out.

"Hey, I thought we were going to *party?*" Bruno said.

"Out," she said. "Now."

He looked from her to Jesse, then slowly slid from the seat with obvious disappointment.

Desiree climbed in and, slamming the door, started the car.

"Don't speed," Jesse yelled over the powerful engine, his words lost as Desiree threw the car into Reverse and, tires squealing, headed home.

Jesse stared after her, figuring he'd at least saved her from Bruno for tonight anyway. He turned his gaze on the man. Bruno was still standing in the bar parking lot, his eyes hard with anger and booze. He was big, with wide shoulders and a blockhead on a thick corded neck.

From the looks of things, his nose had been broken more than once. Jesse suspected he was a bar brawler, someone who liked to fight and throw his weight around. He also had a good ten years on Jesse.

As Bruno advanced on him, Jesse stepped off the bike and pulled out his badge, shaking his head as he held it up. Jesse had done a little fighting himself in the old days. But while the thought of kicking the crap out of Bruno had its appeal, he wasn't in the mood tonight.

"You don't want any of this," Jesse said.

Bruno stopped, seemed to give it some thought, then

turned and sauntered down the street toward the faint glow of neon at the opposite end of the street. Betty's Café.

Jesse pocketed his badge, swung his leg over the bike and started the engine. His body was wired, ready for a fight and it took him a while to calm down.

He roared through town and out onto the open highway letting the darkness engulf him, the air and the night soothed him a little. Still, part of him wanted to take the easy way out, just keep going and not look back. In the old days, Jesse would have been long gone. No goodbyes.

But that was the old Jesse. The Jesse who hadn't settled down, built his own cabin, met a woman who he couldn't quit thinking about, right or wrong.

He turned onto the jeep trail that led to his cabin and drove up through the trees and blackness. He parked his bike in the garage, closed the door and stood for a moment just looking at the cabin with a sense of pride—and awe. Home. He'd never needed it as much as he did tonight. He thought of Maggie standing here last night looking up at it.

Inside the cabin, he headed straight for his studio, shrugging out of his uniform and donning a pair of paint-covered cutoffs. He opened the windows to let in the night air, then turned toward his easel.

For a while, he just stared at the blank canvas, then picked up a brush and began to paint, trying not to think about anything. Especially his conversation with his father. Or the Dennisons. Or Bruno.

Mostly he wanted to forget just for a little while

that he was now a cop. *The* cop in Timber Falls. Or that it was his job to find Maggie and arrest her.

After a moment, he lost himself in his work, in the feel of brush bristles in the paint, the paint on the canvas. The ability had been there for as long as he could remember, first drawing as a boy when he could make something appear on paper with just a pencil. Magic. That's how he thought of it. As if it came from somewhere else, certainly not from him.

A shape started to emerge on the canvas, almost startling him as he realized what he had painted. He stepped back and stared at the partial face and the expression he had captured. Maggie Randolph. Eyes the same rich brown as her hair. Smiling.

He tried to remember if he'd seen her smile like that in the short period of time he'd been around her. No. And yet he knew that when she really smiled she would look exactly like she did in the painting. The smile lighting her face from within. Radiant. Breathtaking.

He put down his brush. What the hell was he doing? This woman could be a murderer on top of everything else.

He glanced at his watch—almost 3:00 a.m. Too late or early for anything but sleep. Unless you were a man who couldn't sleep and you knew that somewhere close by there was a woman…

He quickly cleaned his brush, then went down to his bedroom. He put his uniform back on and strapped on the state issued hip holster, before sliding the gun into place, not wanting to think about needing it. Worse, using it.

Then he headed for his truck. Maggie Randolph wasn't through with Timber Falls. He felt it in his gut. That meant she had to be hiding somewhere nearby. She'd had a tent and sleeping bag strapped on her bike. But neither had been there when he'd chased her earlier.

He considered the direction she'd taken when she'd hit the highway, just before he'd lost her. Away from where she was camped. He'd bet on that.

So he headed south, feeling like he knew this woman. She hadn't been off his mind for twenty-four hours. He'd been tracking her, putting together tiny fact after tiny fact about her, discovering more and more that intrigued him. And worried him.

He knew how she would think because he would have thought the same way were he in trouble...and he'd certainly been there. He'd been face-to-face with the woman only a short time and yet he felt as if he had been waiting all his life for her.

Given who her father might be, that scared him more than he wanted to admit. Fate couldn't be that cruel.

The highway was empty, the night dark. This area of the country was littered with campgrounds, small intimate campgrounds that were completely deserted this time of year. Many of them closed. Because the forest was so dense, she would pick an empty campground to hide in.

The campsite would be as far from the road as possible. There were so many and with no one around, she would feel safe. No, not safe enough. She'd pick a campground that wasn't open thinking no one would look for her there.

Then she'd hide at the densest part of the rain forest. And like a nocturnal animal, she would sleep during the day and do whatever had brought her to Timber Falls under the cloak of darkness.

But after her exploits tonight, she would be holed up by now, trying to get some sleep. She would think she was still safe, that no one would come looking for her at this hour.

No one except a man who couldn't sleep. A man possessed.

Chapter Ten

It was just breaking day by the time Jesse found her. He spotted a single tire track in a muddy spot at the edge of the pavement a quarter mile past the locked gate of a closed campground.

He kept going down the road without slowing, then parked the truck and walked back, hoping for the element of surprise.

Following the track, he wove his way through the dark woods, the sky above him a palette of pastels. As the bike track drew him deeper into the dark woods, he could hear the sound of the MacKenzie River, smell the water mingling with the scent of cedar.

This was the first morning in months that it hadn't rained—at least not yet. A sure sign that spring was coming.

The sky lightened over the tops of the trees as he walked. She'd hidden well. No one would look back in here for her. No one but Jesse Tanner who'd been raised here and knew all the good hiding places from back when he was running from the law instead of enforcing it.

As he moved cautiously through the empty campground, it dawned on him that she might not be alone. That maybe the production manager at the plant had been wrong and that Maggie *had* been with the man.

No, his gut instinct told him she was traveling solo. Whatever mission she was on, she was on it alone. She wouldn't have dragged anyone into this. The man Frances Sanders had seen had to have been chasing Maggie, just like it had seemed. Who, he wondered, was after her? And why?

Jesse was at the farthest point from the highway when he spotted the dark colored tent through the trees. It blended in nicely with the terrain. He wondered if she'd planned it that way. He didn't see the bike anywhere around. Maybe she hadn't returned yet.

Cautiously he moved closer, the rush of the river next to the tent masking his footfalls.

Other than the river, the day seemed unusually quiet as if holding its breath—just as he was doing as he neared the tent.

It was a two-man tent. The flap on one end was open and he could see that the space inside was empty. That seemed odd. He felt a stab of worry cut through him. She wouldn't have left the closure unzipped unless—

He caught sight of her bike out of the corner of his eyes. It was partially hidden in the vegetation a half dozen yards behind the tent near the river.

She was here. Somewhere. Had she seen him approach? Was she hiding? More like waiting to attack him when he got too close?

He moved cautiously toward the bike. If she was

planning a quick escape, she wouldn't want to be far from her mode of transportation.

That's when he saw her. Just a flash of flesh through the trees. He swore under his breath as he saw that she was standing buck naked in a pool of river water, her back to him.

The water pooled around her waist as she sudsed her hair, working quickly in what had to be freezing cold water. Nothing could get him in the river this time of year, he thought with grudging admiration. She was tougher than he was.

He stepped closer feeling the pull of her. She had taken over his life the past twenty-four hours. And now he had her in his sights.

Her back was lean and strong. Her shoulders in perfect proportion with her hips and height. Her skin seemed to glow in the first light of day, glistening from the droplets of water on her skin and soapsuds, only the hint of creamy white breasts at her sides, and he wished that he could paint her just like that. A water sprite at dawn.

He looked away, reminding himself that if he was right about this woman she was off-limits to him. He'd found her but she might always be as elusive to him as she'd been for the past twenty-four hours. The mere thought struck him like a blow.

That's when he spotted her clothing hanging from a tree limb at the edge of the river. He moved toward the clothing as she dipped below the surface of the water, coming up almost immediately.

Eyes closed, she flipped her long dark hair back over her shoulder. It fell in a wet wave, plastering itself to her back. She let out a soft sound, shivered and hugged herself against the cold, one arm over her breasts as she turned, the other hand outstretched reaching for her clothes.

Her fingers touched the now empty limb, felt around, then froze. Her eyes flew open.

MAGGIE SENSED his presence just an instant before she realized her clothing was gone from the tree. She blinked water from her eyes and saw him standing on the rocky shore just inches from her and he had her clothes.

She stifled a cry of surprise and alarm and hugged herself from the cold, hoping he didn't see how scared she was.

He held the clothes out to her and she realized he was trying not to look at her nakedness. He'd probably already seen everything there was to see but she was still surprised and touched by his chivalrous behavior.

She wondered how long he'd been standing there watching her. He was wearing his sheriff's deputy uniform, his expression solemn. There was no doubt he was here in an official capacity. Where was Blackmore? Waiting up on the road?

''Hello, Deputy Tanner.'' Her words sounded much calmer than she felt. Her mind was racing. He'd found her? How?

She studied Jesse Tanner's face feeling emotions that surprised—and worried—her. He was a deputy of the law. He would turn her over to Detective Blackmore. He would have to.

"You must be cold," he said still holding her clothes out to her, keeping his eyes averted.

She *was* cold. Freezing. Her body felt numb from the waist down. She took a step toward him and her clothes afraid she would stumble and seem even more vulnerable. Like being naked in the middle of the river with a cop holding her clothing wasn't vulnerable enough.

Looking away, he held out his free hand to her.

For a moment, she considered ignoring his offer of help. But she knew that would be foolish. Her body ached from the cold water and she had no chance of escape without her clothing.

She took his hand and let him steady her as she climbed over the rocks, all the time working on a plan of escape. All the time praying he hadn't already made some deal with Blackmore that involved the Seattle cop taking her back to the city.

"Nice little town you have here," she said.

He nodded, seeming a little amused, and without looking at her, handed her the bra, the white lacy one she'd been wearing the night she went to meet Norman at the pier. She put it on. Jesse seemed to be staring downstream as if completely unaware of and unaffected by her nudity.

She knew better than that but she liked that he tried damned hard to hide it.

He handed her the shirt.

She couldn't help thinking about his art, about him. He wasn't like Blackmore. A man she would bet would have leered before he drowned her in the river.

"You a local?" she asked, buttoning her shirt and

trying to get some warmth back into her body. She would need to move fast when she got the chance.

"Born just down the road," he said. "I left for a while."

He handed her the white matching lace panties, seeming almost a little embarrassed. She balanced on a rock on one foot to pull them on. He held out an arm to steady her, eyes still averted. She accepted his help again, then held out her hand for her jeans.

He handed them to her and she pulled them on over the panties, buttoned and zipped them.

"Spent some time in Mexico," she said.

He smiled. "My paintings. You seem to know more about me than I know about you."

"Somehow I doubt that," she said. "What made you come back to Timber Falls?"

He shrugged. "I got homesick for something familiar and I missed my family."

"Yes." She certainly knew that feeling. She dropped her gaze, not wanting him to see the tears that suddenly burned her eyes.

"How's the ankle?" he asked.

"Better."

He nodded, turning to face her now that she was dressed.

She pointed to her boots a little farther from the river on the bank. Her socks were sticking out of the top of each boot. He moved out of her way to let her go to them.

If she could have felt her feet, she might have made a run for it. But she had no chance barefoot and she doubted she could outrun those long legs of his even with her boots on.

She sat down on a rock along the bank, feeling the sun rising behind her back, the day growing brighter.

He looked good in his uniform. But she hadn't missed the gun strapped to his hip. At least he hadn't drawn it, wasn't now pointing it at her. But then he might think he had nothing to fear from her.

Didn't he realize she would do whatever she had to if he tried to turn her over to Blackmore? Maybe not.

She slipped on her biking boots, then stood, hands on her hips, feeling warmer. She was still scared but at least dressed she might stand a fighting chance.

"I thought we should have a little talk," he said. "You had breakfast yet?"

"Breakfast?" Was he serious?

"I know a place that serves great pancakes."

She looked down the river for a moment, then at him. "I'd rather not go back into Timber Falls."

He smiled. "Not in the daylight, huh. I had a feeling you'd say that. I was thinking we'd avoid town and go to my place."

She eyed him and looked around, expecting Detective Blackmore to show up any minute. "You come out here alone?"

He nodded.

She studied him. "Why pancakes? Why not just run me in? Or shoot me right here? Better yet, you could have drowned me in the river when you had the chance and no one would be the wiser."

He seemed to flinch, those dark eyes widening in surprise. "I know you're running from something but what would make you think I would want to kill you?"

She shook her head. "Maybe because the last cop I trusted tried to?"

His eyes darkened. "Don't worry. I'm not much of a deputy. I've never killed anyone and I'm hoping I don't have to before this uniform comes off in a couple of months."

"That's supposed to make me feel better?"

He laughed. It was a great sound, deep and rich. It made a humming in her chest like an echo.

"Look," he said, "I suspect you're the kind of woman who seldom needs help, probably doesn't know how to ask for it even when you do. But I think right now you could use some breakfast—and maybe a good listener." He held up both hands as if in surrender. "I've been in trouble a few times myself. I know how hard it is to trust anyone. Especially a stranger. Especially someone in a uniform."

Except he didn't seem like a stranger. She'd felt safe with him. Her heart told her that if she couldn't trust this man, she couldn't trust anyone ever. Suddenly her chest gave as if she'd been holding her breath for days. She fought the tears that stung her eyes. "Pancakes?"

JESSE SMILED and nodded, seeing her relax a little. "An old family recipe."

"Your mother's?"

He shook his head. Not likely. "My dad's. He used to get up every weekend and make pancakes for my brother and me." He smiled at the memory. "I think it was the only thing he knew how to cook at the time.''

She returned his smile but he could still see the tension in her body like a coiled spring. He'd have to keep an eye on her. But the tentative smile had made him desperately want to see a real smile. A smile like he'd painted, a smile like he knew she would smile. Eventually. If he could get her to trust him.

A little voice at the back of his mind warned him he could be all wrong about her. He ignored it. He'd learned a long time ago to live with his heart not his head. It had gotten him into some tight spots that was for damned sure. But it was the way he'd lived his life and he wasn't about to change that just because he'd put on some uniform.

''You have what you took from the newspaper and Dennison Ducks?'' He was still Timber Falls' only deputy and Charity would have his hide if he didn't get her file back. Also he was anxious to see what had been in the locked file cabinet in Wade Dennison's office.

She nodded and he walked with her to the tent. Everything he'd felt the first time he'd laid eyes on her was there and then some. The woman had some kind of hold on him. He hated to think what that hold might be—the one thing that would make her off-limits the rest of his life.

Whatever emotions she evoked in him, that one simple possibility wasn't something he was likely to forget.

''If you don't mind,'' he said, ducking into the tent with her. It was close quarters inside, but he had to make sure she didn't have a weapon stashed under the sleeping mat. "Sorry," he said, after he'd checked and found nothing more lethal than a toothbrush.

She handed him two files both thick, one from the *Cascade Courier*, the other from Wade's personal file cabinet at Dennison Ducks. Wade's file had just what Daisy said would be in it. All the reports from the investigators they'd hired to find Angela and the biggest prize of all, the DNA test results on Wade and an illegitimate daughter he'd had by the family's former nanny.

"Charity will be glad to have these back," Jesse said of the newspaper clippings.

"You know Charity Jenkins?"

He nodded, meeting her gaze. "She's my soon-to-be sister-in-law. She's marrying my brother. The sheriff."

Maggie tensed. "Your brother's the *sheriff?*"

"Afraid so," he said with a smile that he hoped would reassure her. "I try not to hold it against him."

"Tell me why I should trust you?" she asked, sounding scared again.

"Because I make great pancakes and I'd bet you haven't had anything good to eat for a while," he said. "Also, you need my help."

"Do I?" She seemed amused by that. "I thought you just said you weren't much of a deputy."

He laughed. "You've got me there."

They stepped out of the tent. The sun peeked over the treetops, turning the forest to emerald.

"Mind if I ask what you're going to do with me after breakfast?"

Oh, he had all kinds of thoughts on that subject but none he could act on. "After breakfast you can tell me why you had to rob the newspaper and Dennison Ducks," he said.

She eyed him with obvious suspicion. "And then?"

"And then I do everything in my power to help you."

She met his gaze, then nodded slowly. "I believe you mean that."

"I do."

"I need you to promise me something," she said and bit down on her lower lip. She had to know he couldn't make her any promises. "Promise me you won't turn me over to Detective Blackmore," she said, her voice breaking.

She'd said the last cop she'd trusted had tried to kill her. Blackmore? Jesse was in no position to promise her that. Not only was he *the* law in Timber Falls, he could go to jail for aiding and abetting a criminal, if she turned out to be one.

He met her gaze and saw fear flashing like madness in her brown eyes. "I promise."

Her relief was so profound she seemed to sag under its weight.

He reached out and gripped her arm to steady her, shocked by the touch of his skin to hers. He let go as if he'd been burned.

"We'll break your camp and I'll come back and take care of your bike," he said, hoping she hadn't noticed his reaction to her. "I'm going to have to insist that you come with me in the truck. Not that I don't trust you."

"Right," she said but smiled at him. He saw that flicker in her gaze. She wanted to like him. The thought warmed him more than it should have.

BACK AT HIS CABIN, Jesse watched Maggie put away another stack of his pancakes. He'd taken back roads after hiding her bike and thought they would be safe. At least temporarily. He poured them both more orange juice.

"These are the best pancakes I've ever eaten," she said between bites.

"Either that or you just haven't eaten for a while," he said, smiling across the table at her.

She stabbed the last bite with her fork, soaked up the butter and syrup from her plate and popped it into her mouth. She looked up at him. Her eyes were several shades lighter than his own, hers rich with gold and ambers.

He stared into them realizing he hadn't quite captured her eyes in the painting he'd started of her.

"Thank you," she said.

"My pleasure. It gave me an excuse to make them."

"I'm not talking about the pancakes," she said quietly. "But the pancakes *are* amazing." Her smile brightened the entire room.

"Wait until you try my dad's," he said basking in that smile and all the time hoping she'd be around long enough that she'd get the chance. "It's his recipe and he's had years of practice."

"Your mother didn't cook?"

He smiled at that. "She passed on when I was nine." Passed on being a mother.

"Oh, I'm so sorry." Her eyes turned to warm honey. "I lost my mother five years ago. I can't imagine losing her when I was nine. That must have been very difficult for you. Your dad lives close by?"

"Just down the road."

"I envy you." She ducked her head in what he figured was an attempt to hide the depth of her pain. "I lost my father two months ago."

The plane accident. "I'm sorry. You were close."

She looked up again, nodded and seemed to be swallowing back tears.

"Maggie, let me help you."

She got to her feet, scooping up her plate and silverware and taking them over to the sink. "The last man who tried to help me got killed." She rinsed her dish, then shut off the water and turned to look at him, leaning back against the sink as she did.

He stared at her for a long moment, then got up and went to the couch and sat. "I've always found it's easier to start at the beginning," he said. "I haven't read you your rights so anything you say can't be used against you in a court of law."

"If I tell you, I will be jeopardizing *your* life," she said sitting down to face him from the opposite end of the couch.

"I'll take my chances," he said, turning toward her so he could watch her face. "Also the job came with a gun." He saw that she got his humor. What more could a man ask for?

"Detective Rupert Blackmore is trying to kill me. I know that sounds crazy...."

"I've heard crazier stories."

She cocked her head at him. "Well, try this one on for size then. The reason he's trying to kill me is because I'm Angela Dennison."

He nodded.

"You don't believe me."

He wished he didn't. "Why don't you tell me why *you* think you're Angela."

Maggie took a breath and told him everything, starting with the fact that her parents had always told her she was adopted. She told him about the plane crash that killed her father, the conversation Norman Drake overhead just before her father's attorney Clark Iverson was murdered, the phone call from Norman demanding ten thousand dollars in return for proof that her father's plane crash wasn't an accident, her call to Detective Rupert Blackmore and finally what had happened the night at the pier.

"Whoever was behind my kidnapping has successfully kept it a secret for twenty-seven years," she told him. "They thought they were safe. If my father hadn't found out and decided I needed to know the truth..."

"Why do you think he did that?" Jesse asked.

She shook her head. "He hadn't been well since my mother died." Her voice trailed off. "I think he was worried that if I didn't know..."

"That once he was gone, the kidnapper might show up."

"My family is fairly wealthy," she said as if it were some dirty, dark secret she wished she could keep.

Fairly wealthy. He smiled at her obvious understatement. "And you're the only child."

She nodded and met Jesse's gaze. "You knew this already," she whispered, her eyes widening with fear.

Jesse quickly said, "I knew some of it, but not all of it. I ran your bike plate. There's an APB out on you. You're wanted for questioning in both Clark Iverson's and Norman Drake's murders."

She let out a cry and was on her feet. "I didn't kill anyone."

"I believe you."

She stopped moving, stared down at him. "Detective Blackmore was at Dennison Ducks last night. He almost caught me." She moved to the window to look out as if she half expected him to be coming up the road right now. "It's just a matter of time before he shows up on the pretext of taking me back for questioning. If you hand me over to him, I'll never make it back to Seattle alive."

"You're positive the man on the pier was Blackmore? You'd seen him before?" Jesse asked.

She nodded as she turned to look back him. "His photo was in the paper." Her gaze pleaded that he believe her. "He'd been given some award for bravery in the line of the duty. I know now that's why Norman didn't go to the police. He said he didn't recognize the voice of the man who killed Clark Iverson. I didn't believe him. Now I know why he lied."

"You think he recognized Blackmore?"

She nodded and sat down again on the end of the

couch. "When I told Norman that I'd called the detective on the case, he went ballistic. Just seconds later Norman was shot and killed and..." Her voice trailed off. "Just before I rolled off the pier using Norman's body as a shield, I saw the killer. It was Blackmore."

Jesse didn't bother to ask why she hadn't gone straight to the police. Or the FBI. For the same reason Norman hadn't. She feared she wouldn't be believed and with good reason. What did Blackmore have to gain by killing her and the lawyer and his assistant while Maggie had just inherited a fortune.

Her story would spark an investigation. If this cop really was a killer, he was too smart to leave a trail. Instead, the heir who'd just inherited would be the number one suspect.

The plane crash would suddenly be suspect. The facts in Clark Iverson's death and Norman Drake's could be twisted just enough to make Maggie Randolph look like a greedy adopted only child who couldn't wait for her last parent to die to get the money. She had to get rid of her father's attorney because he'd become suspicious and Norman Drake had heard her kill him and was blackmailing her. That would explain the money in her saddlebag and the fact that Norman went swimming with the fishes.

Any other woman and Jesse might have believed it himself. But not Maggie.

"There is something I need to tell you," he said and he saw her tense. "I ran your prints after the newspaper break-in. I suspected Blackmore had inquiries about you tagged so he would know about them immediately. That could be how he found out where you were.''

She shook her head and reached over to touch his hand.

He jumped at her touch, both startled and uncomfortable by it, and jerked his hand back.

If she noticed, she didn't say anything as she was quickly on her feet and pacing again. ''He knew I would come to Timber Falls once he realized I was alive. I'm sure he realized that when Norman's body washed up and mine didn't. He will contact you for help.'' She looked at Jesse for his agreement.

Jesse shook his head. ''If he was going to, I would have heard from him by now.''

She took a shaky breath. ''You think he plans to take care of me himself without involving you?''

''It certainly looks that way.''

She shook her head. ''I just don't understand what it is that he's afraid I'll find out. That I'm Angela Dennison? In that case, it's too late. Or that I'll find proof that he was behind my kidnapping?''

Maggie saw Jesse's worried expression.

''The actual kidnapper is dead,'' he said, obviously hoping to put an end to any thought she might have of looking for the kidnapper. ''He confessed.''

''I read about that in the newspaper articles. The former Dennison Ducks production manager might have stolen me from my crib, but according to the paper he did it on someone else's orders.''

Jesse smiled. ''I wouldn't believe everything you read in the newspaper. Especially in Charity's.''

''Then you think the kidnapper has been caught?''

He rubbed a hand over his stubbled jaw. He hadn't

shaved in at least forty-eight hours. "I didn't say that."

She smiled, relieved he didn't lie to her.

"I'd agree that Bud Farnsworth wasn't the mastermind behind it," he continued. "I think the first step is to prove that you are Angela Dennison. You already have Wade's DNA test results. I've checked and they can be compared to your DNA to determine if you're his daughter, but then you will still need Daisy Dennison's DNA to prove you are Angela."

She stared at him, surprised by something she'd heard in his voice. "You really do believe I'm Angela."

He nodded slowly as if he didn't want to believe it.

Maggie fought to hide her relief. Tears burned her eyes. Dammit, she would not cry. She'd let herself cry only that once in the tent, she wouldn't cry now.

But she hadn't realized how badly she wanted this man to believe her. Needed him to. It validated the risks she'd been taking and so much more. This man who'd helped her that first night on the highway...there was something about him that had kept him in her thoughts ever since.

And that worried her. Just as this feeling she had when she was around him that she was safe. He made it hard to remember that there was a formidable killer after her. She wasn't safe. Would never be safe until Blackmore was behind bars.

And now she'd put Jesse's life in danger, as well.

JESSE SAW a determined look come into her brown eyes.

"I have to find the people responsible before they find me," she said.

"Now wait a minute—"

"You were born here, right? You know these people. I was kidnapped here." She was pacing again and talking fast. "How did Blackmore find me? Did he know this production manager who supposedly took me out of the house that night? And why kill me? It doesn't make any sense to kill to cover up a twenty-seven-year-old kidnapping. But I have to find out."

"Yeah but hold on," he said getting to his feet. "You start trying to get proof of who you are and asking a lot of questions and you'll bring the killer right down on you. You need to go somewhere safe and stay there until I find out who is behind this."

"No way." She was staring him down even though she had to look up to do it. He had her in height, girth and strength and yet he could see that she would take him on in a heartbeat if that's what it took.

"If you're right, Blackmore has already killed three people and wounded you and he almost caught up to you last night," he said trying to reason with her. "You can't take the chance that next time he won't miss."

"You're right," she said, throwing him off guard. "All I would be doing is waiting around for him to find me and kill me."

He told himself she'd given in too easily. There was a gleam in her brown eyes that he didn't like.

Before he could open his mouth, she said, "That's why I'm going to announce to the world that I'm Angela Dennison—and I know the perfect place to do it."

Chapter Eleven

"Rozalyn Sawyer's party?" Jesse exclaimed.

"I saw the ad in the newspaper. Everyone in town is invited. It's the perfect place to make my debut as Angela Dennison," Maggie said leveling her gaze at him, daring him to try to stop her. "The Dennisons will be there, won't they?"

"The ones who aren't in jail."

"Let's start with them then," she said as if it were a done deal.

"You can't be serious. No way."

Her eyes were shiny and bright, her jaw set in stubborn determination. "I'm a target no matter what I do. But once I announce that I'm Angela Dennison at this party one of two things will happen. Blackmore will get out of Dodge, figuring it's over, there is nothing he can do now."

"Or he'll kill you because then he will know where you are and how to get to you."

She smiled and nodded. "Exactly."

"And you think this is a *good* plan?"

"Come on, you know I'm right."

"I know you're suicidal," he said.

"It will be like hiding in plain sight," she argued. "I will be a harder target to hit because everyone in town will be curious about me, right? They'll be watching me everywhere I go in a town this size. I'll be front-page news. Only someone really desperate will try to hurt me with all that heat on me." She smiled. "I'm right and you're starting to see it."

"Yep, it's definitely the fastest way to get yourself killed," he said, but he knew he didn't fool her. She had a good point and as much as he wished otherwise, he was starting to see some merit to her crazy scheme.

"Of course, I wouldn't want to spoil the party so I would do it at the end."

"How very thoughtful of you," Jesse said, hating that she was right. She was already in danger. Announcing who she was wouldn't add to that. Maybe it would even make her safer, although he wasn't counting on it.

"Under two conditions." He held up his hand before she could interrupt. "Keep in mind that I have every right to lock you up in jail if you don't agree."

She clamped her lips shut, eyes narrowed as he proceeded.

"First condition, you never leave my side the entire night," he said.

She rolled her eyes as if to say, "Don't push your luck."

"Second, do you know anything about firearms?"

"Let me see," she said cocking her head to inspect the one he was wearing. "That would be a Glock nine-millimeter, ten-shot magazine, steel slide, double-action trigger, autoload.''

''But can you shoot one with any accuracy?'' he asked, only a little surprised at her knowledge of firearms.

She mugged a face at him. ''I don't happen to have my marksmanship certificate with me but my father used to take me to the indoor firing range and I always hit what I aimed at.'' Her smiled faded. ''I guess Dad thought it was a skill I might need one day.''

So it would seem. ''Shooting at a target is one thing, firing at a living, breathing person is a whole different ball game,'' Jesse said.

''You told me you never killed anyone,'' she reminded him.

He shook his head. ''That doesn't mean I never *shot* anyone.'' He waved her next question off. ''It was a long time ago. I was young and cocky and foolish.''

She studied him openly as if she still found him to be at least two of those. But her look said she didn't find that to be a bad thing. ''This will work,'' she said as if she thought he still needed convincing.

He smiled ruefully. ''I wish I didn't agree with you but it sounds as if Blackmore is already in town. The best way to protect you is as Angela Dennison because you're right, everyone will be watching you. The news will spread like wildfire. And hopefully, it *will* make you a harder target to hit. That doesn't mean he won't try to kill you.''

She nodded. ''He's risking so much, I can't believe he's acting alone. Unless I can find a connection between him and the Dennisons or Timber Falls....''

He groaned. "Which of course you're not going to be doing."

She shot him a look. "I have to find out why I was kidnapped, who was behind it and why they want me dead. You aren't going to try to stop me, are you?"

"I could put you in jail for breaking into two businesses," he pointed out.

She smiled and shook her head. "Then I would be easy pickings for Detective Blackmore. He would try to take me back to Seattle for questioning in Norman's and Clark's murder and I would never make it there alive."

Jesse quaked at the thought. "What makes you think he won't try that anyway?"

"You'll stop him," she said and looked up at him.

At that moment, he would have wrestled bigfoot for her. "You have a lot of confidence in me, more than is warranted, I fear."

"I know you're going to help me find whoever is after me." Before he could argue the point, she added, "And you need *my* help. I'm the only one who can identify Blackmore as the man on the pier who shot Norman and tried to kill me. But I need proof. Unless I can find the connection between Blackmore and my kidnapper..."

He cocked an eyebrow at her. "It's been twenty-seven years. What makes you think you'll find the real kidnapper after all this time? Even if he lived in Timber Falls back then, it doesn't mean he does now."

She smiled. "You don't believe that any more than I do. Blackmore wouldn't be trying to kill me if he thought I couldn't uncover something—and not just that I'm Angela Dennison. There has to be more."

"It's just crazy that anyone would try to cover up a kidnapping with multiple murders."

She nodded. "So the motivation isn't fear of prison for kidnapping charges. It's much more personal and complicated than that."

He stared at her. "What is worse than losing your freedom?"

She shook her head. "That's the way you and I think. Someone else might be just trying to save his skin."

"Like Blackmore."

She nodded. "Or keep their part in the kidnapping a secret because they regretted what they'd done so many years ago and now would lose their family, friends, social standing.... I don't know. Different values for different folks, right?"

Yeah. But he had another theory. Some people cared only about themselves and did what made them feel good no matter how many people suffered because of it.

He realized he was thinking of his mother and when he looked up, Maggie was frowning at him.

"Did you get enough to eat?" he asked as he went back into the dining area to clear his dishes.

"Gobs," she said following him. "I'm going to need something to wear to the party, a drop-dead dress—if you'll excuse the expression—one that won't show that I'm carrying a gun," she said then seemed to realize that she'd never answered his question. "You asked me if I could pull the trigger if someone was intent on killing me. Someone who already killed my father, who for the record was a very kind nice man. A killer who has already tried to kill me once?'' She met his gaze. ''In a heartbeat.''

He saw that she believed it. He prayed if push came to shove, that she could do it to save herself. Because everything about her told him, that like her adoptive father, she was a very kind nice person. And the more he knew about her, the more interested he became in this woman.

He set to work washing the dishes in the sink to quell those feelings. She moved in beside him, opening one drawer and then another until she found a clean dish towel, completely ignoring his, ''I can do these, really.''

''If I couldn't shoot the person after me,'' she said as if he hadn't spoken, ''I wouldn't stay with you.'' She picked up one of the plates and began drying it carefully. ''I know that I'm jeopardizing your life by being here.'' She put the plate in the cabinet and looked over at him. ''You're risking your life because of me. I have to be able to do the same for you.''

''That's the last thing I want.''

''Too bad, because that's the way it is,'' she said and stepped to him, standing on tiptoes. Her lips brushed across his cheek like a sweet whisper, sending sparks shooting along his nerve endings.

He flinched and stepped back.

''Sorry,'' she said looking both surprised and confused.

''You shocked me, that's all. Static electricity, you know.'' He could see the lie reflected in her gaze.

She studied him. "You shock easily."

He laughed, feeling like a fool, and took the dishrag over to the table, putting distance between them, but still intensely aware of her. He could smell the scent of her on his skin, a faint tangerine fragrance that lingered like the memory of her touch.

No woman had ever affected him like this. He told himself it was because he couldn't have her. Might never be able to have her. But he knew it was a hell of a lot more than that or his heart wouldn't ache the way it did at the thought.

"Okay, what's going on?" she asked behind him. "I appreciate everything you've done for me, Jesse. But I feel like there is something else going on between us and I know you feel it, too."

He turned to find her framed in the sunlight spilling in from the window, her hair burnished mahogany, her eyes fired with gold, her hands firmly planted on her shapely hips.

"What is it you aren't telling me?"

Maggie knew she couldn't be wrong about the energy that sparked red-hot between them. "I know you're attracted to me. So what is it? You trust me, don't you? You don't think I killed Norman or—"

"No! I trust you," he said.

"Well, I know you're not..."

"Gay?" He laughed. "No."

She frowned. "Then, I must be wrong about you being attracted me?"

He smiled ruefully and shook his head. "That's not it, believe me."

"Then what? Jesse, every time I get near you, you shy away as if you're afraid for me to touch you."

He met her gaze, his expression pained. "My father had an affair with Daisy Dennison twenty-eight years ago."

She stared at him at first uncomprehending. "You think I might be..." She laughed.

"Sorry, but I don't see the humor," he said.

"It's just that when I realized I was Angela Dennison and that Wade was in jail for shooting the sheriff, among other things, I wished anyone else in the world was my biological father."

"Be careful what you wish for, huh?"

She nodded. "That's why you want the DNA tests." She groaned inwardly. "What if we are half sister and brother?" The thought hurt. She couldn't believe her disappointment, it felt soul deep. Not that she hadn't always wished for a sibling but not Jesse. Not this man she'd wanted since the first time she'd seen him. She trusted him with her life but she wanted more. She wanted to know what it felt like to lie in his arms and—

Suddenly she felt like crying. She hadn't realized until that moment how much she'd been hoping that Jesse would make love to her before she had to announce to the world that she was Angela Dennison and wait for a killer to come after her.

"How quickly can we get these DNA tests?" she asked.

JESSE FELT the cell phone vibrate. "Hold that thought." Once and for all, they would find out who had fathered Angela. They couldn't find out soon enough to suit him. He reached in his pocket, pulled out the phone and saw who was calling. "I still have forty-five minutes before I have to check in," he said to Sissy.

"Trust me, I wouldn't be calling you but Daisy Dennison is demanding to talk to you and I mean now. You think *I've* got attitude?"

"I get the picture." He shot Maggie a look. "Put Daisy through."

"Have you heard the news?" Daisy barked.

"What news is that?" he asked warily.

"Wade made bail!"

Wade made bail? He looked over at Maggie again. Damn, this only made things more dangerous for Maggie until he could find out who was behind her kidnapping. If they were both right and she was Angela Dennison. "When did this happen?"

"Yesterday afternoon. No one notified me. He was released first thing this morning. That means he could be on his way to the house at this very minute," Daisy cried.

"You have a restraining order on him," Jesse pointed out.

"The same one he broke last time when he tried to kill me."

Jesse wanted to point out that his brother wouldn't have been shot and would still be sheriff and handling this if Daisy hadn't provided Wade with the gun. Better yet, if they hadn't been struggling over it. "I guess I could talk to Wade—"

Before he could explain that his hands were tied

until Wade did something illegal, he heard a noise outside his front door. The soft scuff of footfalls on the steps. He tensed and motioned to Maggie to go up stairs and stay hidden and silent.

The knock at the door startled him. He hadn't heard a car engine. Whoever was at the door had walked up the mountain. His first thought was Detective Rupert Blackmore.

As Maggie disappeared up the stairs, he headed for the door, saying into the phone, "Mrs. Dennison, I'm going to have to call you back—" He opened the door. "Daisy."

She smiled, obviously satisfied that she had surprised him. "I'm glad you've dropped that ridiculous Mrs. Dennison stuff," she said, stuffing her cell phone into her purse as she pushed her way into the cabin. "I need to talk to you."

She wore an off-white linen suit. Her purse and shoes were white-and-brown and matched. Her hair was brushed back from her face and she looked younger.

For a woman who'd been a recluse for years, she certainly had become social since her husband had gone to jail.

Jesse closed the door and leaned against it, arms folded over his chest, watching her as she stopped in the middle of the room and looked around.

"You share your father's talents, I see," she said turning to look back at him. His father had built the house Jesse and Mitch had lived in as boys.

"If this is about Wade making bail—"

She waved a hand through the air. "I've decided to

hire a bodyguard since my gun was taken as evidence.''

Jesse lifted a brow. A bodyguard? He guessed he should be glad she hadn't decided to purchase another weapon. ''Do you really think that's necessary?''

''That isn't the reason I'm here,'' she said ignoring the question. ''Is there any news on the break-in at the decoy plant?''

He shook his head. ''Nothing to report yet.'' He hoped Maggie stayed hidden until tonight. Once she made her big announcement all hell was bound to break lose. He wanted to be ready for it. As ready as possible.

He watched Daisy look around the cabin and realized all of this could have been handled on the phone. So why had she walked all this way and in those shoes?

She seemed to see something and headed for the stairs before he could push away from the door and stop her. ''I heard you were painting again.''

''Just a minute—''

She kept going up the wide wooden stairs toward the third floor studio.

He went after her, glad to see his bedroom door was closed as he passed. ''I don't really have anything you can see,'' he said as he took the stairs after her unable to contain his anger. ''It's all at the framer. But you're welcome to come to the show I'm having in June.''

He stopped at the top of the stairs.

She stood in the middle of the room, her back to him. She didn't turn. Nor had she responded to his words. She seemed rooted to the spot, her body rigid.

As he moved toward her, he saw that she had one hand to her mouth. Her face was deathly pale and she was trembling.

He swore under his breath as he realized why she'd come up here. What she'd seen. The partially completed painting resting on his easel. He had captured only a likeness of Maggie, but enough that Daisy must have seen the resemblance to Desiree.

"Daisy—"

She turned. Her eyes welled with tears.

"Daisy?"

She bolted down the stairs. He heard the front door slam.

A minute later, Maggie appeared at the top of the stairs to the studio.

She looked past him at the painting of her, then moved toward it like a sleepwalker. She stared at it for a long moment, making him nervous.

He feared she didn't like it, didn't think it did her justice, that it might offend her.

"You have captured a part of me I've never seen before," she said quietly. She turned then to look at him. "She saw the painting, didn't she?"

He nodded.

And Maggie had seen *her* he realized. "You think she knows it's me?"

"I think it spooked her."

Maggie nodded. "She was definitely upset."

He knew that, like him, Maggie was wondering if Daisy was upset because of the resemblance to Desiree or if she had recognized her other daughter, maybe had known where Maggie was this whole time, had followed her life because Daisy had been the one to get rid of her twenty-seven years ago—and was trying to again. Only this time permanently to protect herself. And she was using Detective Rupert Blackmore to do it.

"Are you all right?" he asked Maggie, fighting the urge to take her in his arms and comfort her.

"It's a shock to see her, in person. I thought I was ready to meet her, but I wasn't."

"You don't have to go through with this tonight."

She smiled at that. "We both know better than that. I can't spend the rest of my life looking over my shoulder. I heard you say Wade Dennison has been released on bail. He's still a suspect, too, isn't he?"

"My future sister-in-law thinks so," Jesse said.

"Charity? She must have good reason to believe that being a journalist."

He smiled at that. "I think it's time you met her and my brother. We'll take along the DNA test results you got from Wade's office. We need to put as many pieces of the puzzle together as soon as we can."

"You know what the tests are going to tell us. That I'm Angela Dennison."

He nodded. "And who your father is. Or at least isn't."

Chapter Twelve

Mitch couldn't believe it. Florie arrived with the news just after daybreak—long before the *Cascade Courier* hit the streets.

Wade Dennison had made bail.

Anyone who hadn't been planning to go to Rozalyn Sawyer's gala party that evening quickly changed their minds, according to Florie. Clearly, no one wanted to miss the fireworks when Wade showed up at the party later tonight—restraining order or no restraining order.

Mitch had to agree there was little doubt that Wade would show up. Wade Dennison *was* Timber Falls and Roz's party was the highlight of the year so far. Plus, if a man was prone to making scenes what better arena than a party with everyone in town in attendance?

''I got scooped,'' Charity bemoaned as she brought Mitch his breakfast tray. The phone had been ringing off the hook all morning as the news spread. ''It's all over the county by now.''

Mitch sat up a little straighter in his recliner. ''I think you're missing what is really important here,

Charity. Wade Dennison has no business being out on bail. He's dangerous.''

''You don't think he'll come gunning for *you* again, do you?''

He smiled at the concern in her voice. ''No,'' he said with a laugh. ''It isn't me I'm worried about. It's you. And Daisy.''

Charity was already shaking her head. ''Wade doesn't scare me and I don't believe for a minute that he tried to kill Daisy. If anything I think she might want *him* dead.''

''Well now that he's out on bail, she just might get her chance,'' Mitch said. He had a feeling this was going to be a long divorce.

And the worst part was, he was trapped in a cast. He'd never felt more useless in his life. He couldn't wait to get back to work. Jesse was capable enough but wasn't really trained for this type of trouble.

Mitch had thought about calling in a state officer, then rejected the idea. Jesse would see that as a lack of confidence in him and Mitch didn't want a rift between him and Jesse, not after all these years of being apart.

No, he just prayed that Wade didn't cause any trouble, but even as he thought it, he knew better. It was almost as if Wade had a black cloud hanging over his head, following him around.

If Wade had anything to do with baby Angela's disappearance twenty-seven years ago, then maybe this was his bad karma coming back to haunt him. Damn, Mitch realized he was starting to sound like Florie.

The phone rang. He reached over and answered it before Charity could do even that for him, then realized it would probably just be another call from gossip center.

"Little brother?" Jesse said.

Something in his tone warned Mitch. "What's wrong?"

"Is Charity there?" Jesse asked. "Can you get rid of her for a little while?"

Mitch could feel Charity watching him. He laughed and smiled. "You scared me." He shook his head at Charity to indicate nothing was wrong, just his brother Jesse being Jesse. "What you need to do is buy yourself a good miter saw. You can use it to cut your own frames after you finish this project."

"She's standing right there," Jesse said on the other end of the line.

"Exactly. Maybe you don't want to cut your own frames now but when you're famous—"

"Would you mind if I went out for a while?" Charity whispered. "Sorry, but I need to stop by the paper."

"Just a minute, Jesse." He cupped the receiver. "Take your time, Jesse is coming over. He's trying to build—"

"You two have fun," Charity said grabbing her purse. "Build whatever you like while I'm gone." And she was out the door.

Charity had heard plenty about the building of Jesse's cabin while it was going up. Fortunately, her eyes glazed over whenever the two of them talked about anything to do with hammers and nails now.

"She's gone," Mitch said into the phone the moment he heard the door close.

"We'll be right over." Jesse hung up.

Mitch stared at the phone in his hand. *We'll* be right over? And whatever it was, Jesse didn't want Charity to know about it. Another bad sign.

CHARITY COULDN'T BELIEVE her good luck. She'd been trying to come up with a good reason to leave the house all day. Mitch had been acting suspiciously, knowing she was on another story—and worried about her. She didn't want to worry him and she knew he would have a cow if he found out who she was going to meet.

Once in the car, she pulled out her cell phone and dialed the number from the e-mail she'd received just that morning.

He answered on the first ring.

"It's Charity. I was hoping now is a good time—"

"You got the message? Good. Yes, come now. You do remember how to get here I assume?" He hung up without waiting for an answer.

Charity took the back way, ditched her car in the woods and walked the last few blocks through the woods to the back of Madam Florie's. As she sneaked around the rear of the former motel, she hoped her psychic aunt was hard at work giving advice to some love-struck woman in Algona, Iowa, or a gambler in Elko, Nevada, and not peering out her window at bungalow uno: Aries.

Aries was one of twelve separate bungalows that had been motor court units, but were now furnished apartments. Florie lived in the main office building and did her psychic business from there.

At Charity's tap, Wade Dennison opened the door and quickly ushered her inside. The furnishings were sparse. A sunken couch with worn cushions, a threadbare overstuffed chair and a cigarette marred coffee table.

She could see through the doorway into both of the only other rooms. A small bath with a sink, toilet and shower stall. A bedroom with a bed and a beat-up chest of drawers. It could have been a rental in any town in the nation.

"It's not much," Wade said with obvious embarrassment. He'd fallen far from the mansion he'd built for Daisy. Charity knew it must irk him that he couldn't go near the place because of the restraining order Daisy had on him.

"Please sit down," he said.

She took the chair he offered. He perched on the arm of the couch. Jail seemed to have made him calmer. Or maybe he just wanted her to think that.

For just an instant, she considered what she'd done. Coming here. Worse, not telling anyone where she was. It hadn't been that long ago that Wade Dennison had threatened to kill her.

"You said you wanted to set the record straight," she said, pulling out her reporter's notebook and flipping it open to a clean page. She snapped her ballpoint pen and looked up expectantly.

If it was a trick to just get her here, she figured now was when he would make his move.

He didn't move. But he did hesitate, then he let out

a long sigh and said, "I'm innocent. I didn't shoot the sheriff."

Another innocent man unjustly accused. "Your fingerprint was on the trigger," she pointed out, hoping this hadn't been a complete waste of time.

"But Daisy's finger was on top of mine," he said. "Daisy is trying to set me up. She's taken my freedom, my home, my business. Daisy called me and said she wanted to see me that night. She planned to kill me. I see that now." His voice broke. "Worse, I think she might have had our daughter kidnapped." He buried his face in his hands.

She wasn't buying it. "Why tell me this, Wade? You've never talked to me about anything."

He raised his head slowly. "I'm desperate."

"As flattering as that is..."

"Haven't you ever considered that I might be innocent?"

She thought that over for a moment. She'd definitely considered it. But right now he looked guilty as sin.

"Why would Daisy have her own child kidnapped?"

"I threatened to throw her out if the baby wasn't mine and take Desiree from her. I knew she had been having an affair—"

"With whom?"

He shook his head. "I didn't want to know. But a man can tell when his wife has been with someone else. I think she was in love with him and I think the baby was his. But I would never have harmed a hair on that baby's head. Never. And I wouldn't have really thrown her out or taken Desiree like I threatened. I think that's why she got rid of the baby, you know, because she was afraid I'd find out the truth and go through with my threat.''

This was a theory she'd actually considered. It certainly explained those years Daisy was a recluse. Getting rid of one child to save another.

''The last time we talked you told me you were convinced Angela was your baby,'' Charity pointed out.

He shook his head. ''I hoped she was. She could have been. There was this one night when Daisy and I...''

She got the picture. ''Was Daisy thinking of leaving you for this other man?''

His expression told her she'd hit the bull's-eye!

''She wouldn't have done that. The only reason we're apart now is that she's mad at me after my illegitimate daughter showed up.''

''Or is she mad because you offered your illegitimate daughter one million dollars to keep it quiet?''

''That wasn't it,'' Wade said getting to his feet. ''I had an affair when Daisy was pregnant with Angela. That's what she's mad about.''

Charity's brain was freewheeling. Was it possible Wade had engineered Angela's kidnapping because he thought it was the other man's baby and he knew Daisy wouldn't leave him with the baby gone?

It was a far-fetched theory, but it made as much sense as any of the others.

''Daisy seems happier now,'' she said. She left off, ''Now that you aren't in her life.''

Wade let out a laugh. "She *has* everything and if her lawyer has his way, she will leave me penniless if not in prison."

"You *shot* Mitch," she reminded him.

"It was an accident. That night was so crazy. I think that's when I realized what Daisy was up to. I know I was acting strangely."

"You almost *killed* Mitch."

He nodded, ducking his head. "I feel terrible about that. That's why I contacted you. I was hoping you'd do some of that snooping you do so well."

She took that as a compliment. "What am I snooping into? The shooting seems pretty cut-and-dried."

"Not that. Angela's kidnapping. Find out once and for all who took that baby and clear my name. I've had this hanging over my head for too many years. When the truth comes out..."

He believed he would be exonerated of everything and would be back in the mansion, back on top? Obviously so. Was it possible he really was innocent?

"You really think Daisy had something to do with it?" she asked.

"I think Daisy might be capable of anything, including getting rid of that baby so I would never find out it wasn't mine."

Charity closed her notebook. "Someone hired your production manager to take the baby out of the house. Did Daisy even know Bud Farnsworth?"

"Of course she knew Bud. But I think she told Bud to get rid of the baby and he gave it to someone else and really didn't know what happened to Angela after that," Wade said.

Charity remembered the night in the plant when Bud had tried to kill her over a blackmail letter that incriminated him in the kidnapping. Daisy had shown up, wounded Bud. What had she kept saying to him? "Where is Angela?" Could Wade he right about her?

"Bud couldn't have gotten into the house without some inside help," Wade said, his voice low. "Someone left the window in Angela's room unlocked."

Charity didn't have much to go on and Wade knew it. The case was ice-cold. Twenty-seven years. And it wasn't like she hadn't tried to solve it from the time she was a kid.

What intrigued her most was this mystery man Daisy had thc affair with. Charity had heard rumors for years. But was this a man Daisy had actually fallen for? Someone she would have left Wade for? Now that was interesting.

THE RESEMBLANCE was unmistakable Maggie thought as she and Jesse entered the back door of the house and she saw the man sitting in the recliner. The same deep dimples, dark hair and eyes, and easy smile.

"Meet my little brother Sheriff Mitch Tanner," Jesse said. "Mitch? Say hello to Angela Dennison."

Mitch's mouth was agape as he stared up at her.

Maggie smiled tentatively.

"How...where..." He shot a look at Jesse. *"Angela?"*

"Looks like a slam dunk but we still need the results from the DNA tests," Jesse said. "We just couriered a batch to the lab in Portland. Albert said he should be able to get us the results in twelve hours. Midnight tonight.''

Mitch looked from his brother to Maggie again. ''I'm sorry to stare but...''

''It's all right. I know I look a lot like Desiree.'' She saw a look pass between the brothers and groaned. ''You aren't telling me that Desiree might also be your half sister?''

''It's possible,'' Jesse admitted.

''You told her?'' Mitch asked his brother in surprise.

Jesse nodded and shrugged. ''Kinda had to.''

''Oh,'' Mitch said, studying him. ''It's like that, is it?''

Jesse grinned bashfully.

Mitch shook his head. ''Other than looks?''

''It all adds up—dates, background, recent events,'' Jesse said.

''I *am* Angela Dennison. I would stake my life on it. Actually I am.''

Mitch frowned.

''Someone's trying to kill her,'' Jesse said. ''A Seattle cop.''

Mitch groaned and leaned back, closing his eyes. ''What the hell is it with this rainy season?''

''There's more,'' Jesse said.

Mitch opened his eyes and narrowed them at Jesse. ''How did I know there would be?''

''The cop is in town. He's killed three other people and tried to kill her, as well.''

''You haven't gone to the Feds?'' Mitch demanded.

''It would be her word against his and he just happens to be an old cop with a lot of commendations, his most recent from the mayor.''

Mitch swore under his breath. ''A Seattle cop? How does he fit into all this?''

''That's what we're going to find out,'' Maggie said making Jesse smile at her determination.

''We don't think he acted alone in the kidnapping. We need to find out how he ties in,'' Jesse said. He quickly filled his brother in on everything. When he finished, Mitch was looking at Maggie with open admiration. Jesse couldn't help but smile since he had to admit his choices in women in the past had left something to be desired.

''So,'' Maggie said when he'd finished. ''We realized the best approach would be for me to announce who I am at the party tonight and see how it shakes down from there.''

''Rozalyn Sawyer's party?'' Mitch cried, echoing his brother's earlier surprise. ''*We* decided? Are you nuts?''

Jesse shrugged. ''I felt the same way when Maggie first came up with the idea.''

''Maggie?'' Mitch asked.

''I was raised as Maggie Randolph,'' she said. ''I'm going to need a dress for tonight. Can your fiancée help me with that?''

''Charity?'' Mitch looked to his brother. ''You aren't suggesting—''

They heard Charity's car pull up out front.

''She's going to hear about it tonight anyway,'' Jesse pointed out.

Mitch was holding his head as if it ached. "Do either of you have a clue what you're about to do?"

Jesse smiled. "*I* have an inkling. Maggie's in for a surprise."

Charity came through the door just then. Maggie hadn't been sure what to expect given the way the men were acting.

A beautiful woman about her own age with a long mass of reddish blond curly hair swept in. She had bright blue eyes and instantly Maggie felt drawn to her.

"You must be Charity Jenkins," Maggie said, going to greet her. "I've read a great many of your newspaper articles. You write very well."

Charity looked both surprised and confused and decidedly curious. As Mitch had done, Charity stared at her as if she thought she should know her.

"I'm Angela Dennison and I need your help," Maggie said.

"Charity speechless. It's a wonder to behold," Jesse said as he took his future sister-in-law's hand and led her to the couch across from Mitch and started to fill her in, as well.

Charity, if anything, was a quick study. "You're the one who stole my file."

Maggie nodded. "Sorry. Jesse has it. I kept all the stories in proper order."

Charity smiled at that and looked to Jesse. "Is she really—"

"We'll have the DNA test results by tonight," Jesse said, "Maggie wants to make her announcement at the party."

Charity looked at Maggie. ''You're using yourself as bait?'' she asked, cutting right to the chase.

''Something like that. I'm going to need a dress,'' Maggie said. ''One that I can hide a small handgun in. Can you help me?''

Charity had been watching Jesse and Maggie while they'd told their story. Now she looked at Mitch and smiled that sly matchmaking smile of hers.

Mitch groaned, knowing it was impossible to stop Charity without telling her that Maggie might be his half sister—and Jesse's. That was one can of worms that would be opened soon enough.

Charity stood. ''Come on. You're about my size. Let's see what we can find in my closet. I live next door. So you and Jesse just met?''

As they went out the door, Mitch shook his head. ''Dad know about this?''

''Yep. He already gave me his DNA test.''

Mitch looked up at him in surprise. ''Then it's possible...''

Jesse nodded solemnly. ''I'm afraid so.''

''This is a damned dangerous plan.''

Jesse couldn't agree more. ''That's why I want you there, carrying. I might need all the help I can get. I don't expect the kidnapper to make a move at the party—''

''You're hoping for some reaction though, aren't you?'' Mitch said. ''How are you planning to protect her after the party? Especially if this Seattle cop is determined to get to her?''

Jesse took a breath and let it out slowly. ''For starters, not let her out of my sight.''

Mitch just looked at him.

"What?"

"You've got it bad for this woman."

"Bro, I can't explain it. That's why I have to get those DNA test results and get my head around however they come out."

"Charity's going to flip when she finds out that I've been keeping this secret for all these years," Mitch said.

Jesse smiled at his brother. "I think she'll still marry you. Anyway, June is a long way off. She might not even still be mad at you by then."

"WHERE ARE WE GOING?" Maggie asked as they left Mitch's and took back roads as they had earlier. She had pulled her hair up into a ponytail and was wearing a baseball cap that Charity had lent her.

"My dad's house. His name is Lee Tanner. He's a good guy. You'll like him."

Her look said she'd make up her own mind about that.

He liked that about her. He liked a lot of things about her. He just wished he knew for sure who her father was if she really was Angela Dennison. Until he did, he'd have to keep her at arm's length. And that was the last thing he wanted to do.

Chapter Thirteen

Rupert Blackmore had brought a tent but the rain changed his mind about camping. He checked into the only motel in town, the Ho Hum. He used cash, but he wasn't worried about being recognized—not with his old pickup, fishing hat and gear.

He liked to think that the only person who knew him in this town was Margaret Randolph and he was looking for her—not the other way around.

Of course he couldn't be sure her kidnapper didn't also know him—just not in this disguise. Nor was the kidnapper expecting him to turn up in Timber Falls, right?

He was pleasantly surprised how small the town was. Finding her should be easy—if she was still around. He figured after him almost catching her last night at Dennison Ducks she would have split. Since she hadn't already gone to his superiors or the Feds, he figured she wouldn't. This could be the end of it. No one in this town would ever have to know of her existence.

He spent the day fishing, keeping his eye out for

her, but deciding to take advantage of where he was. Hell, he might as well consider this a little vacation. Admittedly, he was relieved he wasn't going to have to kill her.

She was rich. She'd return to Seattle. She'd keep her mouth shut. He'd retire and move to Arizona. None of this would ever have to come out.

He'd convinced himself that everything was going to work out as he drove through town, stopping at the gas station. A teenager came out to pump his gas.

Rupert got out of the truck and walked back to the rest room on the side of the building. When he came back out after using the facilities, he saw that the kid was washing his windows so he wandered into the office.

It was one of those old gas stations with nothing more than a counter and a pop machine in the office, an attached single-bay garage and two pumps.

As he was leaving, he picked up a newspaper, leaving thirty-five cents on the counter.

He walked back out to his pickup, paid cash for the gas and sat for a moment as the kid went back inside, paying no attention to him.

His hands shook as he read the story about Daisy Dennison of the famed Dennison Ducks decoys. He remembered the bumper sticker he'd seen on the guy's pickup that night, the night a man he'd never seen before met him in a deserted warehouse parking lot and handed over a wriggling baby wrapped in a tiny quilt with little yellow ducks on it.

He'd put the bundle on the passenger seat, looking up as the pickup and driver took off into the night.

That's when he'd seen the sticker and the muddy Oregon plates. He couldn't make out the plate number. Even then had he planned to find out where the baby was from? Probably. After all he was being blackmailed and now he had a clue who his blackmailer was. A Dennison Ducks bumper sticker on the back of the retreating pickup. Timber Falls, Oregon. Home of the famous decoys.

He pulled away from the service station, reminding himself that he'd been a good cop. Before and even after that one fateful night.

He'd been young, a little too cocky, a little too convinced that he wasn't just going to save the world, he was going to be one of those cops who got commendations all the time on television and in the newspapers.

And he had, despite what happened that night thirty years ago. It was a convenience store robbery and he and his partner were just around the block. They came screaming up in the patrol car just as the perpetrator took off down the dark alley.

Rupert had been the first one out of the car. He ran down the alley. It was so dark. He'd yelled for the perp to stop, heard him climbing a chain-link fence at the end of the alley and in what little light there was, fired.

The pressure had been on him to succeed. He'd found out that Teresa had another guy interested in her, he wanted to look good and prove to her she was marrying the right guy.

He had wanted the bust. Needed it.

But when he neared the fence and the downed body

lying in the pool of blood, he saw that it wasn't the perp at all but a kid of not more than nine, shot once in the back of the head.

He'd been so upset, he'd dropped his gun. It had gone off and shot him in the leg. A freak accident. Unlike killing a nine-year-old boy in an alley. He must have been in shock after that, sick to his stomach, throwing up, barely conscious when his partner found him.

By that time, his weapon was missing. Later he would realize that someone had come in behind him and picked it up carefully from the ground. An opportunist who saw that the gun with his fingerprints on it could be valuable in the future.

His partner, a guy named Wayne Dixon, came upon the scene, saw Rupert on his knees, wounded, bloody and missing his gun and thought that the perp had overpowered him, taken his gun and shot him and the kid.

Rupert had been in no condition to tell him he was wrong. Later… Well later, he'd let the lie stand. Telling the truth wouldn't bring the kid back and would only hurt his career and his chances with Teresa.

She'd come to see him at the hospital. He'd proposed on the spot and she'd accepted.

He put the rest behind him, thinking it was over.

Over until the night he got the call to meet the man in the warehouse parking lot. To get rid of a baby. And the blackmailer would get rid of the gun. He would never be contacted again, he'd been promised by the distorted voice on the phone.

So he'd met the man at the warehouse parking lot,

taken the baby but then the baby quilt had moved and a small cry emitted from deep inside. That had been his mistake, opening the quilt and looking down into that little face. It had taken his breath away.

If there had been any way, he would have taken her home to Teresa. But he and Teresa had only been married a few years and he hadn't known then that they would never have a child of their own. Plus how would he have explained the baby to her? He didn't want her to know about the mistake he'd already made in his life. He would have done anything to keep her from knowing. He still would.

He'd bundled the baby back up and driven away from that warehouse parking lot, heading for Puget Sound, thinking he would get rid of the baby and maybe the blackmailer would never contact him again. That was the deal, wasn't it? And everyone knew blackmailers kept their word.

Right.

But that didn't mean he didn't abhor being blackmailed. He guessed that was partly why he balked at the order and instead of getting rid of the baby in Puget Sound, he sold her to the Randolph's attorney, Clark Iverson. The other reason was the money. He bought Teresa a house. He made some rich couple parents. For twenty-seven years everyone had been happy with the outcome.

And then the adoptive father got sick, stumbled on the truth and decided his daughter needed to know so she could be united with her biological parents.

And Rupert Blackmore, once a good cop, became a killer again.

Not that he ever forgot about the bumper sticker on that pickup. Or the blackmailer. He'd done a little investigative work and found out who the baby was and that she'd been kidnapped. And then he'd let it go, thinking he had a place to start looking for the blackmailer if he ever heard from him again.

A few months ago he'd read about Bud Farnsworth being killed and that he had been the alleged kidnapper. Rupert had recognized the guy in the newspaper article. He was the man who'd brought him the baby. But it had been clear that night that this Farnsworth guy was working for someone else—someone he feared.

Now Rupert Blackmore wondered if Margaret Randolph had seen this story? Would she be so stupid as to knock on the Dennison family door and tell them who she thought she was? Tell them about what had happened at the pier?

No one would be that stupid, especially given the mess the Dennison family was in right now.

He tossed the newspaper on the floor and drove down Main Street toward his motel. Maybe he'd stay around another day. Just to make sure Margaret wasn't still around.

He drove past the sheriff's department. It was little more than a narrow building that shared half the space with city hall. From what he'd heard, the town sheriff had been shot and his brother was acting deputy. The brother had little to no experience, so he wasn't too worried about either of them.

At the edge of town, he pulled into the only café. If Margaret had been stupid enough to go to the Dennisons this morning then it would be all over town by now and he'd been in enough dinky towns to know where to find the gossip in this one.

Still wearing his sunglasses, he parked and went inside Betty's Café, making a point of sitting by the window in the sunlight.

A fiftysomething bottle blonde came out from behind the counter with a menu and a glass of ice water. She set both down in front of him.

"Still got cherry, butterscotch and chocolate pie," she said. "Homemade."

Rupert looked up at her after a cursory glance at the menu. "I'll take a cheeseburger loaded, fries, a chocolate milkshake and a piece of the cherry pie," he said.

She smiled. She wasn't bad-looking, but hey, he was no Prince Charming. And her name tag read: Betty.

"Bigfoot hunting or fishing?" she asked, clearly taking him for a nonlocal.

"I've never heard of Bigfoot fishing," he said flirting with her a little. What the hell? He figured it couldn't hurt. "How exactly is that done?"

She brightened to his smile. "Everythin' bites if you got's the right bait," she said murdering the expression.

He laughed. "I don't care if they bite. I just like fishing."

"That's good because this isn't the best time of year for fishing around here," she said eyeing him.

"But it's quiet and the river isn't crowded."

"Can't argue that," she said and went to place his order.

She came back to the counter where she had a cup of coffee she'd been drinking before he came in.

"I've never been up here before," he said to her and turned to look out at the deserted street. "Is it always this quiet?"

She shook her head. "Everyone's getting ready for the party tonight."

"Party?"

"Sawyers. The daughter, Rozalyn, returned to town and she's throwing a party. Just redid this old Victorian on the edge of the town. You might have seen it on your way in?"

He shook his head.

"It's kinda back off the road. Great old house." She sipped her coffee. "You staying at the Ho Hum?"

He nodded.

"You'll probably hear the party then," she said with a laugh. "I hope you aren't a light sleeper."

He shook his head. "I sleep like the dead."

A bell dinged and she went to get his meal. As she slid the food across the table to him, several more customers came in. They looked like regulars. They glanced at him, took him for what he appeared to be, and sat down.

Outside, low dark clouds scudded past. It looked like it was going to rain any minute.

He ate, listening to Betty talking to the other customers. A no-big-news day. Good. Except for this party tonight. Sounded like the entire town would be there.

He ate his burger and fries and watched the street. No fancy motorcycle went past. No word circulating of a young woman in town looking for her past.

Yep, she'd fled town. He finished off his milkshake, cleaned his plate and started on the pie.

But, he wondered, what would she do next? What could she do? She had no proof. It would be his word against hers. If she couldn't go to the cops and she couldn't run, wouldn't she have to return to Seattle? The woman was rich. Her father had left her dozens of businesses around the world. She would have to return to Seattle eventually.

Sure he'd put an APB out on her, but that was just for questioning in the murders. It was possible he could reach some sort of deal with her. Once she understood that she was only alive because he'd spared her.

Maybe he wouldn't have to kill her. He liked the idea more than he wanted to admit.

And then he would just fade away into the background. Arizona. It was far enough away that she'd feel safe.

He was feeling good by the time he left a big tip for Betty and headed for his motel room. Maybe he'd take a nap and come back later for the dinner special: Pork chops and dressing, applesauce, green beans, mashed potatoes and pork gravy.

The kidnapper would never know that he hadn't held up his end of the bargain.

LEE TANNER came out onto the deck as Jesse drove the pickup into the yard and shut off the motor. Lee's gaze went to the young woman who climbed out. He looked like he'd been cold-cocked with a sledgehammer.

She had that effect on people. Maybe especially on Lee Tanner given how much the woman looked like Desiree.

''Maggie, meet my father, Lee Tanner,'' Jesse said as they climbed the steps to the house.

Lee extended a hand. Maggie took it. ''You're Angela,'' he said. It wasn't a question but she nodded anyway. ''I just finished lunch but I could—''

''We've eaten,'' Jesse said cutting his father off. Charity had cooked up lunch, all the time talking fifty miles an hour with Maggie. Hadn't he known they would hit it off?

''Were you planning on going to Roz Sawyer's party tonight?'' Jesse asked him.

Lee shook his head. ''Why?''

''I thought maybe I could change your mind,'' he said. ''Maggie's going to announce who she really is tonight at midnight.''

Lee lifted a brow.

Jesse grinned wryly. ''Yeah, by then we'll actually know who her father is. We'll still need Daisy's DNA test results to prove without a doubt that she's Angela but I don't expect any surprises there.''

''What can I do?'' his father asked.

''You still have a gun?'' His father nodded. ''I'd like you to come to the party and have it, just in case.''

''This have to do with those murders back in Seattle?'' Lee asked.

''Yeah. There's a cop after her. He's already killed

three others.'' Jesse pulled out the faxed copy of the photo of Detective Rupert Blackmore and the mayor. ''He's the one on the right. It isn't a great photo.''

''I'd recognize him if I saw him but you're not expecting him at the party, are you,'' his father said.

Jesse shook his head.

''We don't think Blackmore is behind the kidnapping,'' Maggie said, speaking up. ''We think it was someone local.''

Jesse met his dad's gaze. ''Someone inside the house left the baby's window unlocked.''

''It wasn't Daisy,'' Lee said. ''It wasn't her.''

Jesse nodded, although not sure of that and wondering why his father was so adamant. ''Well, there were other people in the house that day.'' His mother for one. He hadn't told Maggie about that yet.

''I'll be at the party,'' his dad said. ''Just let me know if there is anything else I can do.''

''Thanks.'' Jesse grinned at his old man. ''I knew I could count on you.'' He turned to Maggie. ''She's also quite capable of taking care of herself.''

Maggie smiled at that.

Jesse shook his dad's hand and watched while Maggie hugged him. He could see the conflicting emotions in his dad's face. Clearly, Lee Tanner wouldn't have minded if Maggie turned out to be his daughter.

Jesse hoped his dad would have to settle for daughter-in-law, but then again that was way down the road and he wasn't sure it was the road Maggie wanted to take. There were fireworks between them and some bond neither of them understood. Until the possibility of shared blood was established or eliminated...

He wouldn't let himself think about it. There were too many hurdles yet to leap. Keeping Maggie alive. Finding out the truth about her biological father. Finding the kidnapper.

Maggie was right about that. She wouldn't be safe until they did.

He watched her walk over to a wall filled with photographs his father had taken of him and Mitch from the time they were babies. She ran her finger over a black-and-white of him.

Jesse felt his father's gaze on him, a look of worry in his expression. His dad knew him too well, knew how much this woman meant to him... How much was at stake tonight.

Chapter Fourteen

Jesse heard a sound, looked up and saw Maggie at the top of the stairs. His heart leaped to his throat. He had never seen anything so breathtaking. So beautiful.

Maggie wore a bright red dress that accentuated every one of her assets. Her dark hair was down and floating over her bare, lightly freckled shoulders.

''You are amazing,'' he said, his voice breaking.

Her dark eyes glowed as she started down the steps, the dress a whisper against her skin.

''You're just saying that because you know I'm carrying a weapon under this dress,'' she said, obviously trying to lighten the mood and maybe feeling a little embarrassed by the fact that he couldn't take his eyes off her.

She had a weapon hidden under that dress all right and it wasn't a gun. It was enough to knock him to his knees just thinking about it.

''You can't tell where, right?'' she asked, looking worried.

He shook his head. ''I would never know you were armed.''

She smiled, pleased.

She wouldn't be using the weapon unless he had failed and the target was closing in. He had no intention of letting that happen. His hope was that Maggie wasn't going to have a need for the gun. Not tonight. Not ever.

She moved toward him like a dream.

He stood transfixed. "You look stunning," he whispered.

She smiled as she took the last few steps down the stairs to him.

He caught a hint of perfume, something exotic that fit her perfectly. Charity's doing.

She touched a hand to his cheek, her brown eyes dark as she looked up at him. Her lush lips were painted a pale inviting pink. They parted in a sigh and he felt his heart do a flip inside his chest, all the air rushed from his lungs and it was all he could do not to take her in his arms and kiss her.

MAGGIE FELT tongue-tied as she looked at Jesse in the tuxedo. Had a man ever been so handsome? And yet it was his dark eyes that captivated her as she moved toward him as if her body had a mind of its own.

She ached to touch him, to feel his arms wrapped around her, to lose herself in his embrace.

Just one kiss. She would have given anything for just one kiss. Tonight she would know if her feelings for him would always be forbidden or if she could have her heart's desire. Just the thought made her forget that there was at least one killer after her, and maybe more after her announcement tonight.

She stepped to him, so close she caught his male scent mixing with the soapy clean smell of him. No aftershave. Just a maleness that made her knees weak. If she even thought of Jesse's lips on hers, Jesse's arms wrapped around her…

"You are extraordinary in that tux," she said, her voice breaking. Everything about him made her blood fire and her skin warm.

When he looked at her with his dark eyes, her heart hammered with a need like none she'd ever known.

"You know how I feel about you—"

He touched his finger to her lips and shook his head. "I know."

She swallowed back the tears that threatened. She wanted him, needed him. She'd known few men intimately. Most had not interested her enough that she wanted to go beyond a few dates.

Jesse had captivated her that first night. His art alone had seduced her. But it was when she'd watched him from the screened-in room, watched him run his hand over her bike that she'd realized she yearned to feel the warmth of his palm on her bare skin, his gentle fingers, the whisper of his skin pressed against hers.

He removed his finger from her lips, his gaze like a caress.

"Jesse," she said on a breath as if that one word swelled with the emotions she felt for him.

He seemed to tense as if he knew what she wanted, what she needed and he felt the heat of this banked fire between them and knew that if they fanned even the slightest ember it would flare and burn blindingly bright, sweeping them up in a maelstrom of passion that neither could nor would resist.

He didn't move. Didn't reach for her. But she could see it was as hard on him as it was her.

"Ready?" he asked, his voice low.

She nodded, unable to speak. She had to be strong tonight, whatever happened with the DNA test results. Whatever happened after her announcement.

"A hug for luck?" she asked softly.

HE'D BEEN AFRAID to touch her, afraid he would be lost. But he opened his arms, knowing that tonight could change everything between them, and she stepped into them and rested her head against his chest, her arms looping around his waist. He closed his arms around her, hugging her tightly as he closed his eyes at the wondrous feel of her. They stayed that way for a long moment, holding each other.

Then she stepped back and he reluctantly let go of her. She smiled up at him. "Show time?"

He nodded and glanced at the clock. Almost eleven-thirty. She would make her announcement at the stroke of midnight—the same time Albert had promised to call with the DNA test results. Another thirty minutes.

The cell phone vibrated in the pocket of his tux. He pulled it out.

"How you holding up?" Mitch asked.

"Okay. What's the news there?"

"Roz just announced her engagement to Ford Lancaster," he said. "Charity's crying tears of happiness.

Roz also did as you requested, announced that she had a special surprise at the stroke of midnight."

"Good. We're on our way."

"Be careful."

"Always." He disconnected and looked at Maggie. "Ready to rock and roll? The stage is set. You're the star performer come midnight."

She nodded. "I have my fingers crossed."

He nodded, knowing she was referring to the DNA test results. "Me, too."

The party was in full swing as they sneaked in the back way. Charity opened the door for them. "Everyone is here," she reported. "Daisy showed up with a bodyguard and you'll never guess who—Bruno. Betty's here, too. Talk about a strange trio."

"What about Wade?" Jesse asked.

"Haven't seen him yet. Roz has a couple of guys outside watching for him. If he shows up, they will detain him until midnight." She glanced at Maggie. "Wow, that dress looks sensational on you." Then she looked back at Jesse and grinned.

"Go on back to the party," he told Charity, not appreciating her matchmaking right now. "We'll be upstairs."

She took off and Jesse watched after her for a moment, hoping the fact that she hadn't spotted any unfamiliar faces was good news.

They took the back stairs, climbing up to the third floor. Music and a cacophony of voices rose from the lower floor of the large old Victorian.

Jesse glanced at his watch. "Five minutes and counting."

Maggie nodded. She didn't look nervous or worried now. He watched her check her gun, then shoot him a grin. He couldn't help but admire her determination. He would give anything to have this night over.

Sneaking out to the stairs, he peeked over the railing and spotted Mitch in a corner in his wheelchair.

Daisy Dennison was indeed in attendance with Bruno and Betty close by. Desiree was flirting with several local guys who hung out at the Duck-In.

Lydia was in a more modern wheelchair than Mitch's, sitting demurely in a corner with Angus looming over her, seeing to her every need.

Roz and her fiancé Ford Lancaster were at the center of the room accepting congratulations. Roz's father Liam was talking to some woman—

With a start, Jesse saw that it was Charity's aunt Florie. She looked so different. Her hair was a warm brown color instead of fire-engine red and it was cut into a cap of short curls rather than being wrapped around her head like a turban. And her eyes didn't have that thick turquoise eye shadow over them, either. Nor was she wearing some blindingly bright caftan. She wore a simple blue dress and she had obviously totally captivated Liam Sawyer. He seemed to be hanging on her every word.

As Jesse's gaze scanned the rest of the crowd, he spotted his father. Daisy looked beautiful. He saw that reflected in his father's gaze and felt a sharp jab at heart level. My God, his father still felt something for the woman. The realization shocked him.

He turned to look at Daisy. Her eyes were locked

with Lee Tanner's across the room. Was this the first time they'd seen each other in all these years?

It was clear that whatever had been between them hadn't completely died.

Just then, the large old grandfather clock began to chime the midnight hour.

"It's time," Maggie said next to him.

He glanced at his watch and nodded. They took the back stairs down to the second floor, then Jesse moved out to the top of the stairs.

The music was louder down here, the chattering crowd a dull roar. Jesse caught Charity's eye. She said something to the leader of the band and the music stopped instantly.

As the grandfather clock finished chiming midnight, Roz called for everyone's attention. The crowd quieted and followed Roz's gaze upward to the stairs.

A hush fell over the huge room below as Jesse held up his hands for quiet.

"There is someone here tonight—" Jesse was interrupted by a disturbance at the front door. Wade Dennison came bursting in, his face flushed. "You're just in time," Jesse said and Maggie joined him at the railing.

A murmur rippled through the crowd.

Maggie smiled down on everyone. "I apologize for interrupting the party. Rozalyn was kind enough to let me make my announcement here tonight with all of you together."

She glanced toward Daisy who was looking up at her in shock. Wade just looked confused.

"My name is Angela Dennison," she announced.

The murmur rose to a roar. And at the middle of it, Daisy let out a cry. Jesse saw her expression. Shock. Then horror. Just before she fainted.

Jesse motioned for silence as the crowd moved back to give Daisy air and Desiree rushed to her mother. Lee had gone to her, as well, and was demanding someone get him a cold washcloth.

"What the hell kind of stunt are you trying to pull, Tanner?" Wade demanded. "That woman is not..." His voice broke. He stared at Maggie, then seemed to shrink back from her as if no longer sure of anything.

"I'm here tonight because whoever is responsible for my kidnapping is now trying to kill me," Maggie said.

Lydia was fanning herself, Angus leaning over her.

Another roar from the crowd. Jesse touched Maggie's arm. He wanted to get her out of here. She'd done what she came to do. Now he just wanted her far away from here and safe.

"I intend to get to the truth. To find out who kidnapped me, who wants me dead now."

The crowd was in an uproar. "Is it really her?" Betty was asking no one in particular. It was as if Angela's ghost had appeared and everyone seemed shaken and excited.

Jesse glanced at his watch. Albert still hadn't called with the DNA test results. But it was time to clear everyone out and get Maggie out of here. He motioned to Charity and she touched Roz's arm.

"Party's over!" Roz announced and she and Ford began ushering the guests out. "Thank you all for coming."

Betty offered to keep the café open late for anyone who wanted coffee.

Daisy had come around. Lee and Bruno helped her up into a chair. She sat looking up at Maggie as if she'd just seen an angel. Jesse knew the feeling.

Desiree stared up at her sister for a moment, then turned on her heel and left, no doubt headed for the bar. Jesse hoped she would be all right. He knew this had to be a shock for her and Desiree had had too many surprises in her life lately.

Lydia was still fanning herself in the corner. Angus was frowning in Jesse's direction, obviously upset that Lydia was distraught. Wade had slumped into a chair on the opposite side of the room from Daisy, his head in his hands.

Liam had offered to take Florie home and as Roz and Ford closed the door on the last of the other guests, Jesse's cell phone vibrated.

"We'll be in the kitchen helping the staff clean up," Roz said as she and Ford left them alone.

"Yes, Albert," Jesse said into the phone as he ushered Maggie into the first room off the stairs. "We're ready for the test results." He met Maggie's gaze, his heart in his throat.

"Okay, here's what we've got. Two matches each, but the two groups don't match."

"In English," Jesse snapped.

"Quite simply, your test and your father's match. Miss Randolph's test and Mr. Dennison's match." Wade was Maggie's father!

"Albert, I could kiss you." Jesse let out a long breath. Maggie's eyes were on him. He let out a howl and dropping the cell phone picked her up and spun her around. As he brought her down, he dropped his mouth to hers and kissed her.

Her arms came around his neck and she pulled him closer, her lips parting, her breath mingling with his. Her mouth was pure sugar, her body soft and rounded and pressed to his. He never wanted to let her go.

Jesse slowly raised his lips from Maggie's, grinned down at her, their eyes meeting, a silent understanding passing between them.

"I guess it's time to make our second announcement," he said.

Maggie's eyes were shiny bright. She smiled ruefully as if like him, she couldn't wait to get away from here and finally be alone with each other.

They descended the stairs finding everyone pretty much where they'd left them. Daisy got to her feet and walked toward Maggie. Jesse tensed.

"You're the woman in the painting," she whispered.

Maggie nodded.

"How long have you known she was alive?" Daisy asked Jesse.

"Until a few minutes ago, I couldn't be absolutely sure she was Angela Dennison," he said. "The DNA sample Wade supplied in the death of his illegitimate daughter matches hers."

Wade had come over to them, as well. He stood looking poleaxed. He didn't notice Lee Tanner slump down onto the couch, his face filled with anguish and relief as he buried his face in his hands.

"I—" Tears welled in Wade's eyes. He stepped to

Maggie and gave her an awkward hug. "We'll find out who's trying to hurt you, who kidnapped you. We'll find him."

"We have to go now," Jesse said, looking over at his brother. Mitch nodded.

"I'll talk to you soon," Wade said, touching his daughter's hair, dropping his hand to hers. Jesse saw her squeeze his hand.

"We'll talk," she said and looked to her mother as Wade left.

"I don't know what to say to you," Daisy said, still looking stunned. "It's just such a shock."

Maggie nodded.

Lydia wheeled up. "Come see me child," she said taking Maggie's hand. "I'm your aunt Lydia. I own the Busy Bee antique shop in town. Promise you'll come see me?"

Maggie nodded and smiled down at her aunt as Lydia and Angus left. "I promise. As soon as I can."

"We have to go," Jesse repeated and took Maggie's hand. He was worried that the longer they stayed, the more chance of an ambush as they left.

Mitch was already wheeling himself toward the back door, Charity at his side when she motioned that she needed to talk to Jesse a minute.

"You might want to keep an eye on Bruno," Charity said confidentially. "I did a little checking on him for a friend. His real name is Jerome Lovelace and he has quite a rap sheet."

"For a friend?"

Charity groaned. "For Lydia, all right? She got this

idea that Bruno might be thinking of robbing the antique store.''

Both Jesse and Mitch rolled their eyes at that, just as Charity no doubt figured they would.

''Don't make me sorry I told you,'' Charity warned.

Jesse laughed. ''I appreciate the heads up, Charity.'' The news didn't really surprise him. He watched his brother and Charity leave. When he glanced back, Bruno was by the front door, eyes hooded. Jesse hadn't heard him say a word all night. But Jesse could feel his eyes on them as they left. Mean eyes.

RUPERT BLACKMORE tried to calm down. He'd been sitting in Betty's Café, having a cup of decaf when the door burst open and the café suddenly filled to overflowing with people—and the news.

Angela Dennison had announced she was alive at the party tonight.

Rupert could barely hear the clamor of voices over the rush of his pulse. Blindly, he dropped money on the counter and, sliding off the stool, stumbled out the door. He doubted anyone noticed him or the way he clutched his chest as he leaned against the side of his pickup.

If he was right, if the kidnapper still lived here in this town, then he knew that Rupert hadn't lived up to his end of the bargain.

What would he do? Turn in the service revolver with Rupert's fingerprints on it? Rupert could see the headlines now. His reputation would be destroyed, he might lose his pension and Teresa. Tears blurred his vision.

He'd have to tell Teresa himself. He didn't want her reading about it in the paper. What choice did he have? None.

It was too late to kill Margaret Randolph. The cat was out of the bag, so to speak. But she'd announced at the party that she was looking for the kidnapper and wouldn't rest until she found him. Worse, she'd taken up with the deputy sheriff.

Rupert was sure he'd covered his tracks well on the recent murders. It was time to go back to Seattle. Retire. Move to Arizona. Maybe if he changed his name…

He managed to get the pickup door open and pulled himself onto the seat, closing the door behind him. He'd left the key in the ignition, not worried about anyone in this town stealing his old pickup.

He started to reach for the key, leaning over the steering wheel as he did. That's when he saw the note. It was taped to the radio. It had his name on it.

He gripped the steering wheel. His heart was pounding so hard he thought it would burst from his chest as he looked out to see if anyone was watching him. No one he could see in the darkness.

Hands shaking, he pulled the note from the front of the radio. The tape gave. It was one small sheet of white paper folded in half, his name neatly printed on the front. Detective Rupert Blackmore.

He opened it and let out a cry as he read the words. "I have your wife. Finish the job. No loose ends." The paper fluttered from his fingers and he grabbed his cell phone from his jacket pocket, his fingers shaking so hard it took him three tries to key in his mother-in-law's number. It was late. Teresa would be in bed asleep. So would his mother-in-law, Marlene. He'd wake them both and feel foolish.

The phone rang and rang.

He felt his heart drop to the soles of his flat feet.

Chapter Fifteen

Maggie watched the dark forest blur by the cab of the pickup, so many emotions racing through her she felt numb. Jesse hadn't said anything since they'd left Roz Sawyer's house.

She watched him look in the rearview mirror for the hundredth time and realized he was worried that Blackmore or the kidnapper might be following them.

She hadn't realized how much had been riding on tonight. The announcement and her biological parents' reaction hadn't surprised her. Her sister Desiree's had. It must have been such a shock to them all. At least her aunt Lydia had welcomed her and that warmed Maggie.

She glanced in her side mirror as Jesse turned onto the road to his cabin. As far as she could tell no one was following them.

Leaning back into the seat, she closed her eyes, remembering the look on Jesse's face when they'd gotten the DNA test results. She smiled to herself, opened her eyes and looked over at him.

He hadn't touched her since they'd climbed into the

pickup. Nor had he said a word. His big hands gripped the wheel as he drove, his eyes on the road or the rearview mirror.

Now that there was nothing keeping them apart had he changed his mind?

He pulled up the pickup in front of the cabin, cut the engine and sat for a moment just staring out at the darkness.

She ached to touch him, to feel his mouth on hers, to lose herself in his arms. Silence and darkness settled over them. He seemed to be waiting for something.

A faint light blinked once, then twice from out in the darkness beyond the cabin.

Jesse seemed to relax and she remembered overhearing Lee Tanner's promise to check out the cabin before they returned. Obviously the flashing light signaled everything was okay and that state troopers were in position. Without looking at her, he opened his door and trotted around to hers, taking her hand but not looking at her as he quickly drew her up the steps all the time watching behind them.

JESSE REMEMBERED Charity's words just before they left Roz Sawyer's house. Charity had been waiting outside and pulled him aside.

"Do you have any idea who she is?" she asked, following his gaze to Maggie as she got into his old pickup.

"She's Angela Dennison."

"She's Margaret Randolph and Margaret Randolph is now head of a huge business conglomerate. She's been running it for months, ever since her father's health began to fail.''

How did Charity find out the things she did? He hadn't asked Maggie about any of that. It hadn't mattered. But now he realized what she was saying. Maggie had a company to run in Seattle. What were the chances she would ever want to stay in Timber Falls?

Charity had leaned in to whisper, ''She's not just amazingly smart, she's incredibly rich.''

What could a woman like Maggie see in a man like him? Especially long-term.

Now as he led Maggie up the steps to his cabin, he feared Charity was right. As long as they'd thought they might be blood-related, they had kept their distance. Now that there was nothing to keep them apart, Maggie might be having second thoughts.

THE MOMENT the door closed, Jesse let out a sigh and turned to look at her. What had Charity said to him as they were leaving the Sawyers? Something that had upset him.

''Jesse, if you've changed your mind—''

He grabbed a handful of her dress and dragged her to him, his big hands cupping her face as he brought his lips down to hers.

''Oh God, I've wanted to do that from the moment we left the party,'' he said against her mouth.

Her eyes filled as she looked up at him, her lips curving into a relieved smile. ''I thought you might be having second thoughts.''

He met her gaze and shook his head. ''You?''

She smiled up at him and circling his neck with her arms pulled him down for a kiss.

When she drew back to look at him, he hugged her tightly to him, his breath against her hair. ''Maggie.'' He said her name as if he couldn't believe this was real.

Then he covered her mouth again, his tongue teasing hers, exploring her mouth, her lips as he swept her up in his arms and carried her up the stairs.

A cry of pure joy welled in her chest. She could feel his heart pounding, in perfect synch with hers.

As the kiss ended, she touched his face, cupping his jaw, and looking up into his eyes. They'd reached his bedroom. He stood her on her feet, his gaze never leaving hers. His eyes were dark with desire and she felt a shaft of heat shoot through her. ''Oh, Jesse.''

JESSE JUST STOOD looking at her in that bright red dress. He'd never seen anything more beautiful. He'd never wanted a woman more in his life. What had he done to get this lucky?

He tried not to think about the future. Thought of nothing but Maggie and this moment he'd prayed for, the moment he could hold her, kiss her, make love to her.

Love.

He slipped one bright red strap from her freckled shoulder. She didn't move, her gaze locked with his as he slipped the other strap down. Her breasts swelled beneath the silken fabric as she took a ragged breath.

''I have wanted to make love to you since the first night I saw you,'' he said, his voice sounding hoarse.

She smiled. "I watched you from the window with my bike. Do you have any idea what you do to me?"

He shook his head. He only knew that this woman had come into his life and it hadn't been the same since. He'd been restless that night, the first time he'd seen her, but that feeling was gone with her here. He couldn't bear to think what it would be like without her though.

He pushed the thought from his mind. Hadn't he always lived life minute to minute? This wasn't a time to be thinking about forever. Not now. Maybe not ever.

"All you have to do is look at me, Jesse, and I melt inside," she whispered and brushed her lips over his sending a quiver of desire spiking through him. "I have never felt so safe, so secure, than in your arms."

He started to tell her that she wasn't safe. Not by a long shot, but she hushed him with a finger to his lips.

"You make me feel things I have never felt before," she said looking deep into his eyes. She slowly began to unbutton his shirt, her fingers brushing lightly over his bare skin as she shoved aside the material and flattened her palms to his chest. A fire swept through him, his blood ablaze for her.

Reaching with both arms around her, he unzipped the dress. It fell to the floor in a whisper. She wore a tiny pair of lace panties, black and in stark contrast to her pale freckled skin. The bra was also black, and her nipples were hard as pebbles against the lace inserts. He groaned at the mere sight. Between her breasts rested a small caliber pistol.

He removed the weapon, putting it down gingerly

on the dresser. He brushed his thumb over one nipple as he did. He heard her soft moan. It fueled the fire in him.

He swept her up and carried her to the bed where he laid her gently down, sliding her panties over her slim hips as he did. He tossed them aside and crawled up onto the bed next to her, slipping the bra straps down and unfastening the front hook.

The bra fell away to expose her full rounded breasts. His mouth dropped greedily to each distended tip, the nipple hard against his tongue. He felt her hands working at the tuxedo pants. The real world dissolved in the distance as in minutes they were naked, wrapped in each other's arms, their bodies one. Alone, safe, together. Nothing else mattered.

RUPERT BLACKMORE realized he was getting too old for this. The climb up the side of the hill had left him weak and breathless. He leaned against the trunk of a large cedar and tried to catch his breath.

He stood listening to the pounding of his heart and the night. A breeze moaned softly in the dense pine boughs overhead and he thought he could hear a stream nearby.

He tried not to think about Teresa, what she'd been told, where she was, what had happened to her. He tried not to let the fear or the anger make him stupid, force him to make a mistake.

He'd already run across one state trooper. The blow hadn't killed the man. Just bought Rupert time. He wondered how many more were in the woods around Jesse Tanner's cabin. How many more he'd have to take down before he finally reached Margaret Randolph.

This felt wrong. All wrong.

He told himself it was because he didn't want to kill the young woman. But he would. He had to if he hoped to see his beloved Teresa again.

He fought back the grief and regret that threatened to completely overwhelm him and concentrated on the terrain in front of him. His eyes had adjusted to the darkness. He moved quietly through the woods, figuring he should be coming up on another state cop pretty soon.

He hadn't gone far when he stopped to listen. A chill rattled up his spine. He'd survived this long as a cop on instinct and right now his instincts were telling him to get the hell off this mountain, too get the hell out of this state. To run.

But he knew he couldn't run far enough. And if he ever wanted to see Teresa again…

He heard the crack of a twig behind him. That's when he knew why this had felt all wrong. He'd been set up.

MAGGIE LAY staring up at the wooden plank ceiling smiling to herself, her body warm, sated. She'd known he would be a wonderful lover. Just the thought made her quiver inside. No man had ever made her heart beat with such fierceness or her body respond with such joy.

But it had been more than physical. She had known that if they were allowed to come together it would be amazing. She still felt awestruck by the feelings he had evoked in her. She loved him. She felt as if she had from that first night when he'd come to help her on the highway.

She listened to Jesse's rhythmic breathing next to her, his thigh against hers, his body still hot from their lovemaking, the scent of him still filling her senses.

Sleep beckoned but she fought it. Being here with Jesse felt so right but she knew it could be taken away from both of them in an instant. For a while she had forgotten about Blackmore. About her kidnapping.

She couldn't give in to this feeling of happiness. Not knowing that the killer hadn't given up. Blackmore would be coming for her. And he might not be coming alone.

Blackmore. There had to be a Timber Falls-Seattle connection. One that she'd missed in the research she'd done. Jesse had picked up the sheriff's department file on her kidnapping earlier and they'd poured over it before the party, but they hadn't found any link.

Where did Blackmore fit in? There had to be some connection.

She slipped from the bed.

"Are you all right?" Jesse said, instantly feeling the loss of her.

She smiled back at him. "I'm just going to check something. I'll be back."

She padded barefoot out of the room grabbing his robe as she headed down the stairs to where he'd put all the information he'd collected. Printouts of stories about Blackmore, the official file on the kidnapping, everything gathered about the original suspects.

She looked through the sheriff's department file

again first. Wade and Daisy's accounts contradicted one another's. Was there something there?

She opened the file Jesse had put together for her on Blackmore. Within a few minutes, she felt Jesse come up behind her.

"Blackmore?" he said reading over her shoulder. He dragged up a chair next to her.

"Look at this," she said, pointing to a photograph taken at one of Blackmore's many award ceremonies where he had been honored for his bravery, his heroism, his excellence as a police officer.

In this particular photograph, Rupert Blackmore was only in his late twenties. He was surprisingly handsome and almost bashful as he took the commendation from the then mayor of Seattle.

"Do you see it?" she asked.

Jesse leaned down to kiss her neck. He took a deep breath, breathing in her scent. Putting his arms around her, he buried his face in her hair. He wished she would come back to bed.

"Look at this," she said.

He pulled back and looked down at the photograph she was pointing at. It was a copy, black-and-white, and the resolution was bad. But he saw that she was pointing at the cutline under the photo, not the men in the snapshot.

He read the cutline hurrying over the list of names. Then reread them, leaning in a little. One name jolted him from any thought of sleep.

Blackmore, Hathway, Curtis, Johnson, Abernathy, Cox, Frank, Peterson. "Abernathy?" H.T. Abernathy.

One of the cops receiving a commendation for assisting in some case.

"There must be a million Abernathys, right?" she asked. "What are the chances he could be related to Lydia?"

Jesse got up and went to find the cell phone. He dialed his brother's number. "I need to talk to Charity," he said when Mitch answered.

"Jesse? Do you have any idea what time it is?"

"Two-twenty-nine in the morning," he said. He could hear his brother call to Charity in the next bedroom.

"Do you ever sleep?" Mitch grumbled.

"Not much."

"It's Jesse," Mitch said. "He wants to talk to you."

"Yes?" Charity said, sounding sleepy as she picked up the extension.

"What was Lydia's husband's name?" Jesse asked her.

"What are you doing playing Timber Falls Trivial Pursuit?" Mitch asked.

"Yeah, strip Timber Falls Trivial Pursuit," Jesse said. "I'm losing so help me out, okay."

Charity groaned. "Don't talk about strip anything, okay? I want a white wedding."

"I admire that about you," he said.

"Yeah," she said. "Henry."

Henry. H.T. "Henry Abernathy?" Jesse repeated, hoping she didn't hear his excitement. "You know what his middle name was?"

"Are you kidding?"

"Okay, what did he do for a living? He owned an antique shop or something, right?"

"Jesse, are you drunk?" Mitch asked on the extension.

"No antiques," Charity said drowsily as if she'd lain back down. "He didn't have anything to do with antiques that I know of. I think that was just something Lydia came up with after he was killed. He was a cop."

Jesse met Maggie's gaze. All the breath had rushed out of him. "Where was that?" he managed to say, afraid Charity had fallen back to sleep she was so slow to answer.

"Bellingham, Washington. Good night, Jesse." She hung up.

"Is everything all right up there?" Mitch asked, sounding concerned.

"Fine. Thanks." He hung up.

"What?" Maggie said on a breath as he put the cell phone on the table by the door.

"Henry Abernathy was a cop in Bellingham, Washington."

"That's not far from Seattle," she said. "It says here they were working on a mutual case. That means they could have known each other."

He nodded, frowning. "But Lydia's husband died before you were born. Even if he knew Blackmore, it doesn't make any sense where you come into this."

"Unless Aunt Lydia also knows Blackmore." She was shaking her head, not wanting to believe it. That little old white-haired lady? She couldn't see her with a man like Blackmore.

''Did anyone mention how she ended up in a wheel-chair?'' he asked Maggie. When she shook her head, he told her how Wade had been driving the car. The night of the accident that killed Lydia's husband and put her in a wheelchair.

Maggie closed her eyes. ''You think she would try to get back at him by stealing one of his children?''

''It sounds crazy to me but some people...''

She opened her eyes and looked at him. ''If her husband knew Blackmore, it's the only link we have so far. She must know him. It's too much of a coincidence.''

He nodded in agreement, obviously not wanting to believe it any more than she did. ''I think we'd better pay Aunt Lydia a visit come morning.''

Maggie rose from the table and went to him, putting her arms around him, just wanting to curl up next to him in the big bed for the rest of the night.

He stroked his hand over her hair and looked into her eyes, clearly thinking something along those lines.

That's when they heard the first gunshot.

Chapter Sixteen

Jesse rushed up the stairs with Maggie at his heels. He dressed quickly and grabbed his gun.

"Stay here." And he was gone out the door. She heard him lock it behind him.

Maggie dressed in jeans, a sweater and boots. She retrieved the small handgun Jesse had given her.

Where was Jesse?

She went to the screened-in deck and stood in the darkness looking down into the jungle of trees and ferns and vines. She couldn't see him. Beyond the screens, a breeze whispered in the pine boughs. Dawn softened the darkness to the east over the treetops. But it was still pitch black in the woods surrounding the cabin.

The moment she heard the two quick soft pops, she recognized them from the night at the pier. Someone shooting with a silencer. Jesse's gun didn't have one so he hadn't fired.

She turned and ran down the stairs, slowing down only long enough to open the front door and ease herself out onto the steps. She waited for her eyes to adjust to the darkness, then with the weapon in both hands, headed toward the place where she'd heard the shots.

She hadn't gone far when she saw the body. Jesse? Oh, God, not Jesse.

Breath left her as she started to rush forward.

''Maggie.'' She swung around, ready to fire. She pulled up short when she saw that it was Jesse.

She fell into his arms, surprising herself by crying. ''Oh, thank God, I thought...''

''It's okay, baby,'' he whispered against her hair as he held her to him.

''Who is it?'' she asked, glancing at the body on the ground.

''Bruno. His real name is Jerome Lovelace.'' Charity had investigated him for some story she was doing.

''The guy who was Daisy's bodyguard at the party,'' she said. ''Is he...?''

Jesse nodded. ''Dead, yes. Shot twice, both bull's-eyes.''

She glanced up at him. ''Blackmore.''

''Whoever shot Bruno, shot to kill.''

She looked into the trees. Still hours before dawn. ''What about that earlier shot?''

''Looks like it came from Bruno's gun.''

She glanced at the weapon lying on the ground next to Bruno.

''It's been fired once.''

She heard a noise and turned, bringing her weapon up.

''Easy,'' Jesse said. ''It's just the state cops. They

were protecting the perimeter hoping to catch whoever fell into the net.''

The state officer looked chagrined since the killer had slipped the net. ''All our officers are fine. We had one down. Hit from behind. Possible concussion. One of the men caught a glimpse of the shooter as he escaped off the mountain. Big man. Older. Possibly wounded. Limping. He got away.''

Blackmore.

Back at the cabin, Jesse checked to make sure they were alone while the state boys took care of Bruno.

''Why would Blackmore kill Daisy's bodyguard?'' Maggie asked.

Jesse shook his head. Nothing made any sense. He picked up the cell phone and called Mitch.

''This better not be trivia again,'' his little brother warned him. ''It isn't even light out yet.''

Jesse heard a soft click on the line as Charity picked up the extension. ''Bruno, aka Jerome Lovelace, is dead. Two slugs. Killer used a silencer. Bruno might have wounded the shooter, but he got away.''

Mitch swore.

''Either Bruno came up there to kill Maggie and someone whacked him before he could,'' Mitch said. ''Or—''

''Or he was here to kill someone else and got himself whacked,'' Jesse said.

''Did I mention where Bruno was originally from?'' Charity asked making it known she was on the line. ''His last known address was a post office box in Seattle, but I found an old car registration in his glove box—''

Jesse heard Mitch swearing in the background.

"And he used to live in Plentygrove not far from where Daisy was originally from," Charity finished.

"Thanks, Charity. Talk to you later, bro." Jesse hung up and looked at Maggie. Plentygrove? "We need to take a little trip."

"Are we going to talk to Lydia?" she asked.

"There's something else I need to do first." He'd only put it off because he became involved with Maggie. "We're going to pay my mother a visit."

Maggie frowned. "But I thought your mother was dead?"

"She left my dad when Mitch was six and I was nine. She's been dead to me ever since."

Maggie raised a brow. "And you suddenly have an urge to go see her?"

"She was at the Dennison house on the day of the kidnapping," he said. "And it seems my mother lives in the same town that Bruno hailed from. Maybe it's a coincidence but I have to wonder what brought him to Timber Falls. Certainly not the weather."

ALL THE WAY off the mountain, Rupert Blackmore could think of only one thing. Murdering the person who'd set him up. The person who had his wife. The person who'd been responsible for Angela Dennison's kidnapping. The person who'd blackmailed him.

He'd listened to enough gossip at the café to know who the obvious players were. But he'd found in his career that sometimes a man had to look behind the obvious.

He drove back into town, went to his motel room

and took a shower, bandaging the flesh wound to his leg. He knew better than to run where Bruno had shot him. The state cops would have the roads out of here blocked. And he wasn't ready to leave anyway.

He called one of his snitches.

"Do you have any idea what time it is, man?"

"Just listen." He opened the wallet he'd taken off the man who'd been sent to kill him. An amateur. "Find out everything you can for me about a man named Jerome Lovelace and I need it yesterday." He gave him his cell phone number, hung up and began to go through Jerome's wallet.

RUTH ANNE TANNER had remarried a guy named Art Fellers and lived in an older part of Plentygrove. That had been all the information his father's lawyer had been able to get on her but it was enough to provide Jesse with an address.

It turned out to be a one-story ranch built in the 1950s, but well kept up. It was late morning when he and Maggie walked up the sidewalk to the front door. The lawn had been cut recently and someone had planted geraniums in matching pots on each side of the door.

He rang the bell and waited. Inside the house he could hear music. He was trying to place the song rather than think about his mother when the door opened.

Jesse had thought she'd look older, be gray, maybe even fat. He definitely didn't expect her to be pretty anymore. But the woman who answered the door had a cap of dark hair that was only flecked with gray and she was slim, athletic-looking. She wore a cap-sleeved T-shirt that matched her Capri pants and white sandals. Her face was unlined, the only wrinkles were around her eyes as she squinted into the sun peeking through the clouds to see them.

"Yes?"

This woman didn't look almost sixty. She was pretty and he realized, she looked happy.

Bitterness tore at his insides. "Hello, Mother."

Her eyes widened and she gripped the door, leaning into it as if she needed the support. She blinked either because of the glare or because she was trying to place him and didn't know which son he was.

"Jesse, but I can understand how you might have forgotten."

Her gaze shifted to Maggie and she seemed to regain her earlier composure. "Please, come in." She moved back and as much as he didn't want to, he stepped into her house after Maggie.

The house was clean and cool inside, the furnishings nice but not expensive.

"Jesse." Her eyes welled and she looked away as she wiped the tears at her cheeks. "Would you like something to drink?"

"Nothing—"

"I'd take something cold if you have it," Maggie said and followed Ruth Anne into the kitchen. "I'm...Maggie."

Jesse followed, just wanting to get this over with.

The kitchen was clean and cute. There was a photo on the fridge of a bald man with his arm around Ruth Anne at some party.

Obviously she'd left Timber Falls and made a new life for herself. He'd always imagined her alone, bitter, hateful, spending his father's money on booze or drugs.

Maggie touched his arm and he took the glass of iced tea she offered him.

''Please, sit down,'' his mother said motioning to the breakfast nook.

''This isn't a social call,'' Jesse said more sharply than he'd meant to. He took a sip of the drink, his throat dry, his nerves raw.

''Do you mind if I take a look at your garden?'' Maggie asked and didn't wait for an answer as she opened the patio door and stepped out, closing the door behind her.

Jesse waited for his mother to say something. Like she was sorry. Right. Could he ever forgive her? No. How was Mitch? What did she care. He thought she'd at least ask about his life.

She didn't. She sat down at the table, folded her hands in front of her and seemed to be waiting.

He wanted to yell at her. To tell her how badly she'd hurt him, his brother, his father. To ask why. To make her feel guilty.

But instead he heard himself ask, ''Did you have anything to do with Angela Dennison's kidnapping?''

She leaned back in her chair, her eyes clouding over as if the name forced her to return to a place she'd left far behind, something seeing him obviously hadn't done. ''She was never found?'' She sounded surprised by that.

He realized he had her eyes and felt an ache in his chest.

Tears welled again in her eyes and her lower lip trembled. ''I can't explain the woman I was when I—'' She made a swipe at her tears, as one coursed down her cheek, and shook her head. ''I didn't take the baby. I never even saw her. As I was leaving I passed the nanny. She had come down the stairs. She had a cold,'' his mother said as if just remembering that detail.

All that had been in the sheriff's report. ''Did you see anyone else in the house other than Daisy and the nanny?''

She shook her head. ''Wade came home. I passed him on the road. His sister was with him in the car.''

''Lydia?'' he asked in surprise. That hadn't been in the file.

''Why are you asking these questions now after all these years?''

He looked past her to Maggie standing by a row of huge sunflowers. ''That woman out there is Angela Dennison. Whoever kidnapped her is determined to kill her.''

Ruth Anne winced and looked through the patio doors at Maggie. ''She is beautiful. She looks like Daisy.'' She slowly shifted her gaze to Jesse. ''And her father?''

''Wade,'' he said.

She nodded. ''Good. I'm sure you're relieved since you're obviously in love with her.''

Jesse got to his feet, angry that she could know

anything about him. "Do you know a man named Jerome Lovelace? He goes by Bruno."

She shook her head, seeming distracted. "Your father... I always hoped he and Daisy would get together," she said as she stood.

He stared at her. Was she serious?

Maggie came back in and he ushered her toward the front door.

His mother didn't try to keep him any longer. Didn't ask about his life or Mitch's or their father's.

"Goodbye, Jesse," Ruth Anne said at the door. She smiled and nodded as if pleased by him.

He didn't say goodbye, just stepped out the door, but he couldn't help himself. He turned to look back at the last moment before the door closed. That's when he saw it behind his mother. One of his paintings on the wall in her living room.

The door closed and she was gone again.

"Are you all right?" Maggie asked and took his hand.

He nodded, surprised that he was. "She seems happy. She was so miserable with us."

"People change. She wasn't even yet your age when she left, right?"

He nodded surprised that he could no longer feel hate for the woman he'd just seen. "She made a lasting impression on Mitch and me. I didn't think Mitch would ever ask Charity to marry him he was so scared of marriage. I'm thirty-five and I've never been serious about anyone before."

She looked away. "I used to wonder what normal families were like."

He laughed. "Me, too. Think there are any?"

"She had your painting on the wall," Maggie said and looked over at him. "She hasn't forgotten you or your brother. She just couldn't handle things at that time of her own life."

He nodded. "I guess I wanted her to say she was sorry."

"Would the words really have made that much difference?"

He shook his head. "She did tell me something about the afternoon of the kidnapping. She said she passed Wade coming home when she left. Lydia was with him."

"Her name keeps coming up," Maggie said.

"It's just strange that it never came up in the sheriff's report that Lydia had been out there that night," Jesse noted. "How did she get home? Did Wade drive her or did Angus pick her up?"

"You think Lydia might know something?"

"It's worth asking her." Jesse realized Lydia could provide an alibi for his mother. If Ruth was telling the truth, then Lydia had seen her leave *before* the baby disappeared.

And what if Lydia had looked in on Angela that evening? She might have been the last person to see Angela before she was kidnapped.

"Let's not forget the possible connection between her now deceased husband and Blackmore," Maggie said.

Jesse shook his head. He hadn't forgotten. So far, it was the only tie-in they had between Blackmore and Timber Falls.

Chapter Seventeen

Rupert Blackmore found only one thing of interest in Jerome ''Bruno'' Lovelace's wallet.

A business card. It was worn and soiled as if it had been pulled out a lot and there was writing on the back, hard to read notes.

He looked at the front of the card. The Busy Bee, Antiques and Collectibles. Proprietor Lydia Dennison Abernathy.

His cell rang. Teresa. But it wasn't Teresa, just as he knew it wouldn't be. His source had come up with information on Jerome Lovelace, a small-time offender from Seattle via Plentygrove.

There was only one offense that Rupert found interesting. The fencing of stolen property. The property in question had been antiques.

He'd learned a long time ago that cases had threads, threads that directed you where to go.

He studied the card, following the thread, following his gut instincts.

Abernathy? He rooted around in the drawer of the

motel's bedside table for the phonebook. It was so small and thin he missed it at first.

Abernathy. Why did that name sound so familiar?

IT WAS DARK by the time they returned to Timber Falls. Jesse called Mitch as soon as he was close enough to town to get a signal on the cell phone.

He told Mitch what Maggie had discovered about Henry Abernathy and a possible connection to Blackmore.

He didn't mention that he'd seen their mother. "I also stumbled across a note that revealed Wade brought his sister home the night Angela was kidnapped. Maggie and I are headed there. We're almost to Timber Falls."

"Lydia was at the house that night?" Mitch said. "Why didn't she say anything years ago?"

Good question.

"Jesse, be careful."

Jesse had just clicked off the phone when he heard a loud pop an instant before the front tire blew.

"Get down!" he yelled at Maggie as he wrestled the steering wheel, fighting to keep the pickup on the road.

He shoved Maggie down as the windshield shattered with the impact of a second shot. The other front tire blew an instant later.

The pickup careened down into the ditch, still moving too fast. Jesse saw the tree coming up and tried to brace himself in that instant before the pickup crashed into it and the lights went out.

"JESSE!" Maggie cried, sitting up.

He was slumped over the steering wheel. She could see blood on his forehead.

"Jesse!" Still stunned from the impact, Maggie touched his shoulder, shook him gently. He didn't respond. She fought to get her seat belt unhooked. Jesse needed her. Her mind raced. She had to get him help. Get help. Someone had shot at them. Someone—

Her door burst open. Rough hands grabbed her and dragged her out of the pickup. She screamed and fought. A strong hand clamped a cloth down over her mouth. Something nasty-smelling on the cloth. She tried not to breathe, wriggling and fighting to free herself from the unyielding arms that held her.

She took a breath. It was the last thing she remembered.

JESSE WOKE to the smell of smoke. His first thought was Maggie. The house was on fire. Get Maggie out.

Only he wasn't in the house. He sat up, blinked at the wetness in his right eye. He lifted his hand to his forehead. It came away wet and sticky. Blood?

He glanced around, confused. He was bleeding and his head was killing him. He was in the pickup, behind the wheel and yet he could smell smoke, feel the heat of the blaze.

"Maggie?" The pickup was empty, the passenger-side door closed. Maggie was gone. Gone for help? Where—

He heard the clank of a door sliding closed and looked out through the thickening smoke, through the spiderweb around the bullet hole in the windshield and saw the blue van, glimpsed the familiar logo on the side.

Panic and pain rocketed him forward. It all came back in a flash. The sound of a shot seconds after the front tire blew. The windshield shattering. Another shot, another tire. Then the ditch. The tree coming up fast. Then blackness.

He seemed to be moving in slow motion. He unbuckled his seat belt and tried to open his door. Jammed.

He scrambled across the seat to the passenger-side door and tried to open it, then saw that someone had jammed a tree limb against it. Had jammed both doors he realized, trapping him inside.

Flames crackled, smoke roiling upward, making it hard to see. *Maggie.* Whoever was driving that van had Maggie. He felt it at gut level, heart level.

He managed to get his gun out of the holster, steady it with both hands as he saw a figure shrouded in smoke come around the back of the van toward him.

He raised a foot, kicked out the already shattered windshield and fired. The figure veered back behind the van, disappearing.

A whoosh and flames flared in front of him.

Jesse began to wriggle through the hole where the windshield had been. He heard an engine rev. The van tires squealed on the pavement.

Sprawled on the hood of the pickup, he raised the gun again but knew he couldn't fire for fear that he might hit Maggie.

Flames leaped all around him, the smoke so thick

the van seemed to dissolve in it as the vehicle roared away.

Get out of the pickup. Now!

He slid off the hood, hitting the ground at a run. Blood ran down into his eyes. His head felt as if it would burst.

Behind him he heard another whoosh. The explosion, as the gas tank blew on the pickup, knocked him to the ground, knocked the air out of him.

He rolled over to look back at the pickup. It was a ball of flames. Past it, he saw the gas can at the edge of the woods, saw where the gasoline had been poured around the pickup and set on fire. The killer had planned for him to die in the pickup, burn to death.

What did the killer have planned for Maggie?

The thought terrified him. He had to get to her first.

He had the cell phone out of his pocket. He wiped a sleeve across his eyes and punched Redial. Mitch answered on the first ring.

RUPERT BLACKMORE left his pickup at the motel and walked downtown. He took the dark side streets, staying to the shadows.

He was a block and a half away from the Busy Bee when he heard the sound of an engine. He stepped into a doorway, flattening himself to the dark entry.

As the vehicle passed, he saw that it was a van, dark in color with something printed on the side. All he caught was the word "antiques."

The van slowed a good block before the shop,

pulled in front of an underground garage. The driver got out and disappeared inside the building.

Rupert waited only a moment, then moved toward the van.

MAGGIE WOKE to darkness and the smell of old wood. She tried to move. Couldn't. Not even a finger. She was lying on her back on something hard and she could tell that there was something around her, close, something solid as if she were in a box.

The thought filled her with terror. She fought not to breathe too fast for fear she would use up all the oxygen inside the space, but she knew she was failing.

She couldn't move her head, but cut her eyes to each side, saw little fissures of light leaking in at the edges of her vision.

She realized she could hear. She opened her mouth and tried to call for help. No sound came out.

Was she paralyzed? The pickup. She remembered crashing into the tree. Jesse?

Her pinky finger brushed against something rough. Wood. She heard a sound. Footsteps. A metal door rolled slowly open next to her. Light. Through the crack at each side of her vision, she caught the flicker of a flashlight beam.

Her body was lead. Only her little finger moved. She tried to scratch the side of her prison but it made only a faint noise.

She heard the groan of springs, felt herself tilt a little as someone stepped next to her. She was in a vehicle of some sort. The realization surprised her. Also scared her. Was she going to be transported somewhere?

She heard the soft scrape of something being moved

next to the box she was in, felt the vehicle rock again, then smelled it.

Her heart stopped in her chest and if she could have, she would have cried out. Stale cigar smoke.

CHARITY WAITED to put down the phone after Mitch so he wouldn't know she'd been on the line and heard everything. She'd been working in the spare bedroom on this week's edition but now she went into the living room where Mitch was on the phone to his father.

"Honey, I'm going to take a shower," she whispered, pretending she had no idea what was going on.

He smiled and waved to her in acknowledgement. She headed for the large bathroom he'd added at the back of the house. The one right next to the back door.

It was crazy. But then she'd done worse for a story. She turned on the shower, then slipped out the back door. She couldn't very well take her VW. Mitch would hear her start the engine.

So she walked the three blocks to the Busy Bee. The light was on in the back. She knocked and waited, her hands in her pocket. One gripping her loaded Derringer. The other clutching the small can of pepper spray.

She hoped Jesse was wrong and that Lydia could explain—

The door opened. Charity hadn't even seen Lydia come out of the elevator at the back. Maybe she'd been in the shop. Sitting in the dark?

A chill rippled over her as Lydia opened the door.

"Charity! I was just thinking about you," Lydia said. "Come in. Come in."

Charity stepped inside the darkened shop, thinking this was probably the worst idea she'd ever had.

RUPERT SHONE his penlight into the back of the van. It held a half dozen pieces of furniture, an armoire, a cedar chest, a vanity, a chest of drawers and the most unusual piece of all, an old Chinese coffin by the door.

He thought he heard a scratching sound like mice. He froze. God, he hated mice. When he was a boy a mouse had run up his pant leg. The memory even after all these years made him break out in a sweat.

He started to back out, slowly, staying low, keeping the penlight on the floor, just in case one of the mice came after him.

He was just about to step off onto the loading ramp next to the side door of the van when he heard it.

Breathing. It was coming from the coffin.

MAGGIE WAITED for him to open the box and kill her. Instead, she heard him let out a curse, heard the rustle of fabric, then heard him standing over her.

The lid groaned and something metallic rattled. A padlock. The box was padlocked shut. Her heart raced as she listened to him try to open it. Didn't he have the key?

The padlock rattled again. Then silence.

Her left hand began to tingle as feeling came back into it. She could move her little finger of that hand now and several more fingers on her right hand but she couldn't lift her arm.

He must have given her a drug of some sort that paralyzed her body but not her mind.

Oh God, what had he done to Jesse?

Feeling was coming back into her body. She just had to remain calm. Time. She would be able to move if he gave her a little more time.

He was still standing over her. She could hear him breathing.

Then she heard another sound. This one in the distance. Footsteps. Someone was coming! Jesse?

Closer, a metal door slid quietly shut, then movement near her, the sound of furniture being moved, then stillness.

The footsteps beyond her prison were coming closer. A car door opening. The vehicle rocked and seat springs groaned. A door slammed closed. An instant later, the engine started and she was moving again.

''WHERE'S ANGUS?'' Charity asked as she stepped inside the Busy Bee and the door closed behind her. ''I didn't see the van.''

''It's his day off,'' Lydia said. ''He went to a movie in Eugene, but he didn't take the van. It should be parked in the garage. Why don't you keep me company until he returns. I just put on a pot of tea and I have cookies. I thought you might be stopping by.''

Charity followed Lydia to the elevator, telling herself that Jesse had been mistaken about the van he'd seen. Or someone had stolen it. Or—or it wasn't really in the garage and Lydia was lying.

The elevator opened on the second floor directly into Lydia's beautifully furnished apartment.

Like a sleepwalker, Charity followed the older

woman as she zipped in the wheelchair through the living room to the kitchen and large dining room.

The teapot was whistling as they entered the warm kitchen. A plate of cookies had been put out. Lydia proceeded to pour them both a cup of tea.

Charity watched her closely, afraid she might put something in her tea. But Lydia made the tea just as she always had and smiled as she handed Charity a cup.

Charity took the seat at the table Lydia indicated and set down her tea.

"Here dear, have a cookie. I know you can't resist my cookies."

JESSE SAW lights coming up the highway, recognized his father's pickup and rushed up the road to meet him.

"My God, son," Lee said, as Jesse climbed in.

"The Busy Bee," Jesse said. "Take me to the Busy Bee. Hurry."

His father spun the pickup around in the highway and took off toward town. Jesse filled him in.

"Mitch said Lydia should be alone at the apartment. It's Angus's day off. He always goes into Eugene on his day off," Lee told him.

"In the van?"

Lee shook his head. "Usually that BMW Lydia bought him."

"Then who has the van?"

Lee shook his head. "They probably leave the keys in it. You know how people are in Timber Falls."

He knew.

"What do you want me to do?" Lee asked.

"Drop me off. I'll take the back. You watch the front. Don't come in unless you hear gunfire."

Lee nodded as he neared Timber Falls. "I love you, son," he said as he slowed and Jesse jumped out, running down the street to the back of the Busy Bee.

Jesse was almost there when he saw the van up the street. The taillights flashed. It was leaving!

The van started to back up. But then as if the driver had spotted Jesse, the van pulled forward.

Jesse started to grab for the cell phone in his pocket to call his dad when he saw where the van was going.

RUPERT COULDN'T SEE the driver. He'd hidden behind a large piece of the furniture that blocked him from the driver's view, as well.

He thought the driver would leave town. Maybe take Margaret Randolph somewhere out in the woods to kill her. But he heard a large garage door clank open and when the van moved, it didn't move far. The garage door clanked down and Rupert realized the driver had pulled into the underground garage. That was odd.

The engine shut off.

Rupert held his breath as he slipped the gun from his pocket to his palm. He was wedged behind the armoire. While he hadn't been able to see the driver, he could see the antique coffin and he could hear breathing still coming from inside. Just like the scratching noise he'd heard.

He waited.

The side door of the van slid open. He felt the van

rock as someone stepped in. A man. Large from the way he rocked the vehicle.

He felt rather than saw the man bend over the coffin and worked a key into the padlock.

Rupert waited for the *click* of the padlock opening. Waited for the man to slip the padlock from the hasp.

Click. Click.

Silence. He heard the man rise slowly, warily, and knew he'd either been spotted or sensed. Either way, he had to move. And quickly.

MAGGIE LISTENED as someone bent over the box she was in. The padlock rattled. She could hear him breathing. Jesse!

No, not Jesse, she realized with a sinking heart as she heard the person insert a key into the padlock. It was whoever had put her in here.

She prepared herself for when the lid opened, willing her arms to work enough that she could fight him off. But first she would lie perfectly still. Let him think the drug was still working. That she was no danger to him.

The lock clicked open. Her heart leaped to her throat. Light. Air. Out of this horrible box.

That's when she heard the first gunshot. A boom that echoed like a cannon blast in the small space almost deafening her.

With all her might, she shoved at the lid of the box, flinging it open.

Another gunshot. Something large fell, rocking the

vehicle. She heard a curse and a groan. Then the lid of the box was slammed shut again as something heavy fell against it.

RUPERT HAD stepped out from behind the armoire and seen the man turn. Something metallic flickered in the man's hand.

Rupert had been struck by the fact that he'd never seen the man before. Somehow he'd expected his blackmailer to be someone he knew.

That instant of surprise was his first mistake. Not pulling the trigger more quickly was his second.

The knife blade glimmered in the dull light. Long and slim. As it shot through the air and buried itself to the hilt in his chest.

Rupert had gotten off two shots.

And then as he fell forward, he saw Teresa in his mind coming toward him, toward the aquamarine pool next to their RV. She had a cocktail in both hands and she was smiling.

"Everything is going to be all right now that you've retired," he heard her say. "Didn't I tell you you would love Arizona?"

THE BUILDING was an old warehouse with a loading dock and underground garage. Jesse thought it was empty, abandoned. All the windows were covered with weathered sheets of plywood crudely painted with No Trespassing.

But as Jesse pried a piece of plywood from one of the windows, he saw that someone had been using the place and for some time.

The first floor was filled with antiques. Good stuff.

Tons of it. He slipped in, dropping to the floor and moved as quietly as possible through the pieces to the stairs that led to the parking garage.

That's when he heard the shots.

CHARITY TOOK one of the cookies, but didn't take a bite. "Lydia, I know you were at the house the night Angela was kidnapped."

Lydia looked up in surprise. "Who told you that?"

"It doesn't matter. It's true. A while back you told me the nanny overheard Wade and Daisy arguing. But it was you. What about the baby? Did you go up to her room?"

Lydia looked down into her cup. "It was a horrible row just like I told you. Wade and Daisy thought I'd left, thought Angus had already picked me up. I knew Daisy had been having an affair. I didn't want my real niece growing up with some bastard's child." She met Charity's gaze.

"What did you do, Lydia?" Charity whispered, her hand dropping to the pepper spray in her pocket.

"You haven't eaten your cookie, dear. Angus made them especially for you." Lydia's hands had been on her lap. Now she produced a gun from under the knitted throw draped over her lap. "I've always told people how you can't resist my cookies. You wouldn't want to make a liar out of me, would you?"

AT THE SOUND of the gunshots, Jesse rushed down the stairs into the underground garage. The blue van was parked just inside, the side door open.

At first all he saw inside were more antiques. There

had to be a small fortune in antiques in this warehouse. What the hell?

Then he saw Blackmore lying at the back of the van, his chest a red bloom of blood, his eyes wide and dead.

An armoire had been knocked over. Jesse straightened it to get to Blackmore, pushing it off the coffin. To his amazement and horror, the lid of an antique Chinese coffin began to rise and there was Maggie.

"Jesse," she whispered, the word barely audible.

He shoved back the lid of the coffin. Her movements were jerky and she couldn't seem to use her legs. Oh God. He swept her up out of the coffin and carried her around to open the door and placed her in the front seat of the van.

"Baby, are you all right?" he cried.

Maggie nodded, her head jerky, her body awkward, at odds with itself. "Drugged. Wearing off," she whispered. Her voice was hoarse, her throat hurt. She managed a smile and she thought he would break down and cry as he rocked her in his arms. She looked over his shoulder, suddenly afraid. "Where—"

"Blackmore's dead in the back of the van." He pulled away to look at her. "How did you—"

She was shaking her head. Or at least she thought she was. "Not Blackmore. Someone else."

He tensed. "Who?"

She shook her head and then her eyes widened in alarm as she caught the glitter of steel. "Knife!"

Jesse spun around, using the van door as a shield. The knife hit the door and clattered to the concrete floor.

He had his weapon drawn again but he could see nothing in the dark corners of the garage. He glanced up, saw the large overhead light. If he could get to the switch.

"Can you lock your door?" he asked Maggie without turning around. He heard the soft snick of the lock as his answer.

He reached over and slid the van door closed and locked it.

He used his boot toe to move the knife closer, but he didn't dare bend down to pick it up. He kicked it back under the van and, locking and slamming the van door he'd used as a shield, moved fast toward the garage door.

In the blind darkness, he raked a hand down one side of the wall. No switch. Rushing to the other side, he did the same.

He heard the noise behind him. Shoe soles on concrete, then cloth on concrete. The killer was under the van, going for the knife.

Jesse found the light switch. Jerked it down, knowing as he did that he would provide the killer with the perfect target. As the overhead light flooded the garage with a dingy gold glow, he leaped to the side, crouching at the end of a tool bench.

Where was the killer?

MAGGIE COULD FEEL life coming back into her body, but she was still so weak.

She watched, feeling helpless, a horrible feeling for a woman who'd never needed help before. She thought of her mother. In a wheelchair all of those years and yet not helpless. Strong. Courageous.

Tears wet her eyes. She watched Jesse disappear into the darkness at the edge of the lit garage.

Where was the man with the knife? The man who had killed Blackmore?

She glanced over and saw the keys dangling from the ignition. Moving awkwardly, she slid over behind the wheel. She started the van.

Suddenly a face appeared at her side window, startling her. She let out a shriek. Angus tried the door, swore when he found it locked.

She threw the van into Reverse, swinging it around. Angus leaped out of the way. She saw Jesse come out of the dark, the gun in his hand. But Angus was facing her. She caught his expression.

She shifted the van into First and gunned the engine as she let her foot up off the clutch.

Angus had the knife in his hand and was turning when she hit him. He went down, disappearing under the hood of the van. But the knife was already in the air. It whizzed past Jesse's head missing him only by a breath.

Then Jesse was at her door. She opened it and he took her in his arms and he rocked her, his breath damp against her neck.

"EAT YOUR COOKIE," Lydia said calmly. "Angus put a special ingredient in it, just for you."

Charity stared down at the cookie in her hand, then at the gun Lydia had pointed at her.

"I wouldn't eat that cookie, if I were you," said a voice behind Charity.

Relief washed over her at the sound of Lee Tanner's voice. He moved into her view. He held a gun in his hand and it was pointed at Lydia.

"I'll shoot Charity," Lydia said not seeming all that surprised to see him.

"It's over, Lydia. Angus is dead."

Her gaze shifted to him, tears suddenly welling in her eyes. "Angus?"

In that instant, he stepped to her and jerked the gun from her hand. She didn't fight him.

Charity dropped the cookie in her hand, swearing off sugar cookies for the rest of her life.

"Not Angus. I can't lose another man I love," Lydia said. "He's such a good man. Just like my Henry. You know Henry was a cop."

"Yes, Lydia, I know," Lee said.

"It's all Wade's fault," Lydia said. "Angus never forgave him for putting me in this chair and killing our Henry. Then when Wade married that tramp and we thought she'd had another man's baby...."

"Daisy isn't a tramp," he said.

She looked up at him. "It was you, wasn't it?"

Charity looked at her soon to be father-in-law.

"You were the one Daisy was in love with," Lydia said and let out a soft laugh. "Why didn't I see it before?"

Epilogue

Jesse stood in the art gallery, the bright sun shining in through the windows.

Spring had finally come to Timber Falls. Mitch had mended and taken over as sheriff again. Jesse had turned in his uniform and his gun and had gone back to painting.

But he didn't kid himself. Everything had changed. Maggie had come into his life. He'd almost lost her. And then, she'd left again.

He hadn't seen her in several months now. She'd had to return to Seattle. Her father's businesses needed tending, she had a house to see to and was needed to testify in the murders of her father, Clark Iverson and Norman Drake.

"Don't worry," Charity had told him. "She'll be back for my wedding. Maggie wouldn't miss my wedding."

Jesse wasn't so sure about that. He hadn't been able to reach her for the past few weeks. Her assistant at company headquarters said she was out of the country and wasn't sure when she'd be back.

The last time they'd talked he felt frustrated. He needed to hold her, to talk to her in person, so he hadn't had much to say. Now he regretted it, wished he'd told her how he felt. Even long distance.

"Son," Lee Tanner said coming up to rest a hand on his shoulder. "Your art show is a tremendous success. You should be proud."

His first big show. He couldn't believe that most of the paintings were already marked Sold. "Thanks."

Lee studied his son. "Have you heard from Maggie?"

He shook his head. "She has a lot on her plate right now." The truth was, there really wasn't any reason for her to return to Timber Falls and Jesse knew it.

Timber Falls had quieted down. There hadn't been a bigfoot sighting in months. Nor a murder. Angus Smythe was dead. Lydia Abernathy behind bars awaiting trial for kidnapping, blackmail and multiple murders.

Before his death, Detective Rupert Blackmore had left a detailed account in his motel room at the Ho Hum of what had happened thirty years ago in a dark alley and the blackmail that had resulted in it.

It seemed Maggie owed her life to him. Not once, but twice.

Blackmore had saved her that night in the garage. His wife Teresa and her mother were found unharmed. They'd been detained by a policeman back in Iowa where Blackmore's mother-in-law lived, and held overnight in a jail cell. It wasn't until the next morning that the policeman realized he'd been sent a false arrest warrant for the two.

Charity had been so sure that Bud Farnsworth was trying to tell Wade who'd hired him to kidnap Angela just before Bud died. If that was the case, then Bud had been trying to tell Wade that it had been Lydia, Wade's own sister.

Over the weeks since, the story had been hashed out at Betty's Café for hours on end. Rumors had been running rampant, as was Timber Falls' style.

Most everyone in town believed that Lydia had become embittered after the accident and was set on getting even with her brother and that's why she'd kidnapped Angela. Others believed Lydia did it to spare her brother the embarrassment when it came out that the baby wasn't his.

Whatever had motivated Lydia, Wade had hired her the best lawyer his money could buy. But then he didn't have much money. Daisy was going through with the divorce. It was rumored there was a new man in her life. In fact, several people had seen her with Lee Tanner.

The general consensus was that it was nice that the two had found each other especially after what they'd both been through.

The antiques Angus had stored in the warehouse turned out to all be stolen. It seemed Angus had been working with a man named Jerome "Bruno" Lovelace for years. Lydia was right about one thing, Angus was quite wealthy in his own right. And he'd left it all to his favorite step-niece Desiree. She had gone away to college but she'd called Jesse before she left.

"You are the one person in town who will appreciate this," she said. "I took a DNA test. I guess I've always known but I wanted to be sure, you know, after everything that happened. You and I...''

''You're my sister,'' he said.

She laughed lightly. ''You knew, too.''

''I figured. You were too wild, too much like me,'' Jesse said.

''I guess we'll all have to get together one of these days, you, me and Maggie,'' Desiree said.

Jesse knew Maggie would like that. ''Let's do that.''

''I guess you know about our parents,'' she'd said before she'd hung up. ''I'm okay with it. Wade, well, he's talking about leaving town. I think it's the best thing. Mom's taken over the decoy plant. Who knew she had it in her?''

Lee Tanner turned now as Daisy came into the art gallery. Jesse couldn't believe the change in his father. His step was lighter. He was definitely happier.

It was good to see Liam Sawyer with Florie, too. Roz and her fiancé Ford Lancaster had also stopped by and bought one of the paintings.

As Jesse looked around the gallery, he was glad to see how many of the locals had turned out. Timber Falls was an okay town. He would hate to have to leave it. That, he realized would be up to Maggie. If she still wanted him.

He noticed that only one of his paintings hadn't sold. It was one he'd done of a Mexican cantina. In it a young woman was dancing and the men at the bar were watching her. He noticed that someone had put a Hold sticker on it.

And then he turned. How had he known it was her?

Maybe the way the air seemed to contract. Or his heart kicked up a beat. But there she was standing in the doorway. Maggie. And he knew then who'd had the painting put on hold.

She moved to him, hesitant at first. She must have seen his expression because she broke into a smile and ran the last few steps, throwing herself into his arms.

"I thought I would never get home," she said.

"Home?" he echoed, holding her close.

She pulled back and looked up at him. "I'm never leaving you again Jesse Tanner. Never."

He heard his brother's voice behind him. "Ask her to marry you, fool."

Jesse laughed and looked down into Maggie's brown eyes, losing himself in them. He'd wanted her from that first night, had been waiting for years for her to come into his life. He couldn't believe how kind fate had been to him. Florie said it was written in the stars.

He figured heaven did have something to do with it.

"I'd planned on something a little more romantic..." he said, then cleared his throat. "Will you marry me Maggie Randolph?"

"Tell her you love her, fool," Mitch whispered behind him.

"We could have a double wedding," Charity said.

"Shush," Lee Tanner told them both. "He's doing just fine."

Maggie laughed, glanced around the room at all the people waiting to hear her answer, then she smiled up at Jesse. "I love you, too, Jesse Tanner. Marry you? Absolutely."